## "Do you know how rarely I drink three glasses of wine in a row?" Greer asked.

"But then, home's right next door," Ryan observed. "And thanks to the wine, you're going to sleep terrifically tonight."

"This is embarrassing." Her feet just didn't want to get into synchrony, and one hip bumped Ryan's.

"What's embarrassing? You're not trying to impress a bunch of high-class company. We're neighbors."

Greer obediently slumped her head against his shoulder. "That's right." She yawned. "Just neighbors."

She sounded ridiculously happy at the thought. Thoroughly irritated, Ryan paused at her door and had a short internal debate with his conscience. His conscience lost. He didn't really intend to take advantage of her, anyway, but they had to clear up this little difference of opinion on neighbors and . . . neighbors.

PAPERBACK
EXCHANGE
131 Vesta
Reno, Nevada 89502
WE SELL - WE TRADE

Other Second Chance at Love books by
**Jeanne Grant**

**Jeanne Grant** is a native of Michigan, where
she and her husband own cherry and peach
orchards, and also grow strawberries. In ad-
dition to raising two children, she has worked
as a teacher, counselor, and personnel manager. Jeanne began writing at age ten. She's
an avid reader as well, and says, "I don't think
anything will ever beat a good love story."

Dear Reader:

October is here—and so are the newest SECOND CHANCE AT LOVE romances!

Kelly Adams has a special talent for endowing ordinary people with extraordinary warmth and appeal. In *Sunlight and Silver* (#292), she places such thoroughly likable characters in a dramatic love story set in America's heartland, on the Mississippi River. Riverboat captain Jacy Jones comes from a long line of women who know better than to trust high-handed men. Joshua Logan comes from a privileged background of wealth and breeding that's always set him apart. The battle of wills between these two *very* independent people sparks sensual shock waves that rival the currents in the ol' Miss!

Few writers create characters as warmly human and endearingly quirky as Jeanne Grant, winner of the Romance Writers of America's Silver Medallion award. In *Pink Satin* (#293), voluptuous lingerie consultant Greer Lothrop feels more comfortable playing the role of resident housemother to new neighbor Ryan McCullough than acting the femme fatale. But Ryan isn't about to accept chicken soup in lieu of tender loving kisses. Once again, Jeanne Grant demonstrates her superlative skill as a teller of love stories in a romance you'll treasure.

With the emotional honesty and sensitivity she is fast becoming beloved for, Romance Writers of America's Bronze Medallion winner Karen Keast touches our hearts with a story of forbidden love between divorcée Sarah Braden and her ex-husband's brother, cartoonist Cade Sterling. While she never shrinks from complex emotional issues, Karen dazzles us with her skillful use of male viewpoint, her lyrical prose—*and* her humor! I can't sing the praises of Karen Keast and *Forbidden Dream* (#294) loudly enough!

*Love With a Proper Stranger* (#295) by Christa Merlin is a powerful love story with an element of intrigue that will keep you breathlessly turning the pages. Anya Meredith doesn't think she's a candidate for a whirlwind romance, but Brady Durant teases and tantalizes her until she impulsively surrenders to passion. Yet when Brady is linked to a mystery surrounding an antique music box, Anya's trust in her lover is severely shaken. Don't miss this gripping romance written by the author of *Kisses Incognito* (#199).

For Anglophiles everywhere, Frances Davies's frolicsome pen creates an unabashedly romantic British drawing-room comedy (at times it's a little like a French bedroom farce, too!), complete with a cast of lovable eccentrics—including the hero, dazzling romance and mystery writer Andrew Wiswood. With witty one-liners and flights of sheer poetry, Frances whisks us to heather-covered Yorkshire and immerses us in whimsy. *Fortune's Darling* (#296) is a sophisticated, delectable romp.

In *Lucky in Love* (#297) Jacqueline Topaz once again creates a bright, breezy romance that will make you feel good all over. Cheerfully unconventional exercise instructor Patti Lyon is willing to bet she can take the starch out of staunch civic leader Alex Greene. But Patti's game-show winnings and laidback lifestyle don't convince Alex to support legalized gambling. In the bedroom he's mischievously eager to play games . . . but elsewhere he intends to show her there's more to life than fun and frolic!

Until next month, enjoy! Warm wishes,

*Ellen Edwards*

Ellen Edwards, Senior Editor
SECOND CHANCE AT LOVE
The Berkley Publishing Group
200 Madison Avenue
New York, NY 10016

*Second Chance at Love*

# PINK SATIN

## JEANNE GRANT

**SECOND CHANCE AT LOVE
BOOK**

PINK SATIN

Copyright © 1985 by Jeanne Grant

All rights reserved. No part of this publication may be reproduced or transmitted in any form or by any means, electronic or mechanical, including photocopy, recording, or any information storage and retrieval system, without permission in writing from the publisher.

Requests for permission to make copies of any part of the work should be mailed to: Permissions, Second Chance at Love, The Berkley Publishing Group, 200 Madison Avenue, New York, NY 10016.

First edition published October 1985

First printing

"Second Chance at Love" and the butterfly emblem are trademarks belonging to Jove Publications, Inc.

Printed in the United States of America

Second Chance at Love books are published by
The Berkley Publishing Group
200 Madison Avenue, New York, NY 10016

# Chapter One

WITH A LAZY yawn, Greer leaned over and peered through the window of the oven. Filet mignon would have been nice, but in a pinch she'd settle for Lean Cuisine.

Straightening, she unbuttoned her salmon crepe blouse and slipped it off, draping it over the nearest kitchen chair. She was broiling. Either her apartment's new temperature-control system was playing games again, or North Carolina's April heat had managed to seep inside, even this late in the afternoon.

Twisting the oven dial to WARM, she wandered back to her bedroom with one hand on the side zipper of her cream-colored A-line skirt. In a moment, the linen garment was gracing the bright tulip pattern of her comforter. *Pick it up, Greer.*

1

She not only picked up the skirt but hung it up as well, feeling abnormally virtuous. The feeling was rare and didn't last long. Once she'd peeled off her stockings, she let them lie exactly where they fell on the poppy-red carpet. One could be good for only so long. Her workday had been both long and unusually tedious.

Halfway to the closet for her white cotton robe, Greer caught a glimpse of her reflection in the dresser mirror. There was nothing strictly wrong with the chartreuse slip she was wearing . . . except that one required sunglasses to appreciate its fluorescent brilliance. Her dresser drawers were full of expensive lingerie with equally minor flaws—sort of a fringe benefit of working for Love Lace.

The flamboyant satin slip cupped a well-developed pair of breasts, pinched in for a miniscule waist, and then swayed alluringly over rounded hips and long, slim legs. There was no excess fat, just luxuriant curves that would have made a calendar photographer deliriously happy. Greer, as usual, scrunched up her nose at the reflection in passing.

If she'd had her choice, she would have been flat-chested and tiny. If Greer's mother had had the choice, her daughter would have had the poise and presence of a svelte Greer Garson. Neither had had her choice.

Nature had endowed her with a voluptuous body and a certain shyness—an unfortunate combination, in Greer's view. As a teenager, she'd been avidly pursued by more than her share of hormone-happy boys. Other girls had envied her; Greer had suffered a lot from mortification. If the boys had just looked above her neck, they might have noticed she was simply an average nice-looking girl, with myopic but sensitive big brown eyes and a mop of untamably curly hair. But boys that age weren't too interested in anything above a girl's neck.

She'd discovered since that middle-aged "boys" still looked below the neck first. Living out her days as a sex symbol didn't hold much appeal for Greer. Actually, it held none. So by the age of twenty-seven she had a degree in psychology behind her and had perfected the fine art of survival. Men and Greer coexisted just fine these days.

Slipping into an ancient cotton robe, she padded barefoot back through the living room. *"Down,"* she called automatically as she picked up a magazine.

Truce was perched on a curtain rod. The tiger-striped feline peered down at Greer with limpid yellow eyes.

"Down, and this time I mean it," Greer warned. "You know what you did to the curtains last time."

The cat ignored her. Greer sighed. Way back, when she had first adopted Truce, he had mounted an assault on all climbable things. *Then* Greer had had high hopes that they could reach an amicable agreement—hence the name Truce. *Now,* Greer understood that cats loved outright war because they always won.

Experienced in the fine art of guerrilla warfare, Greer wandered past the blue and white flowered couch and the mountainous pile of mail on the desk to the window, where she leafed absently through the pages of *Psychology Today.* Presently, the cat leaped down onto Greer's shoulders and curled himself around her neck with a thunderous purr.

Reading as she walked, Greer aimed for the kitchen, automatically groping for a knife and fork in the silverware drawer, then pouring herself a glass of milk. Bending down, she filled Truce's bowl with cat food. The cat continued to wave his long tiger tail in Greer's face, unmoved by the sight of his dinner. "I'm out of gourmet brand and I'm not going to the store until tomorrow," Greer said firmly. "You haven't even tried this. It's tuna fish."

Truce licked her ear.

"Mmmm," Greer coaxed, mimicking a sound of ravenous hunger.

Truce waved his tail.

"All normal cats like seafood," Greer informed him. Truce popped down to the floor and sauntered over to the counter by her purse, clearly expecting his mistress to race to the store immediately for his favorite brand of cat food.

"Whatever happened to gratitude? Can't you even *try* to remember that you were a mangy, starving orphan a few months ago?" Pulling open the oven door, she reached in with pot holders for her dinner. Lasagna.

The phone rang in the living room. A shock wave shivered down Greer's spine; she dropped a pot holder, burned her finger, and turned pale, all in the space of a second. The phone rang again. Nursing her burned finger in her mouth, Greer closed the oven door with a snap and felt her heart suddenly ticking like a time bomb.

On the third ring, she took her finger out of her mouth and starting shaking it, her steps joltingly stiff as she walked to the telephone. Inches away from the receiver, her hand suddenly turned independent, refusing to pick it up. Insistently, the telephone rang again.

Taking in a huge lungful of air, Greer grabbed it. "Hello," she rasped.

On the other end there was nothing. Just . . . breathing.

Greer's fingers tightened around the receiver. "Hello?" she repeated, louder this time.

More breathing. Basically normal breathing. Two

weeks ago, her caller had had a cold, and his breathing had carried a wheeze. Greer had suggested he take a cold capsule, because back then she'd still been trying to deal with her crank caller with humor and patience. Sometime in the interim, all of Greer's normally irrepressible humor had deserted ship.

Well aware her fingers were trembling, she dropped the receiver back into its cradle. Her small apartment, so chock full of cheery colors and familiar things, suddenly seemed to close in on her. The walls echoed silence and a forbidding emptiness. Fear licked along her bloodstream.

*Look. There's nothing to be afraid of. We've been through all this before . . .*

Yes. Rationally, Greer gathered up Truce, her silverware, and her TV dinner in organized fashion. Then, irrationally, she fled out her apartment door.

The hall was deserted, just one harmless front door and four equally harmless steps leading up to the two first-floor apartments. When Mrs. Wissler lived next door, Greer had generally taken sanctuary in her neighbor's kitchen after one of her telephone calls and stayed there until the shaky feeling passed. Unfortunately, Mrs. Wissler had moved three weeks before. Except for Greer, the whole building was deserted. The two single men in the upstairs apartments were rarely home on a Friday night.

She didn't need anyone to hold her hand anyway. What good was a degree in psychology if it didn't help you deal with a simple problem in a logical, rational manner?

Still mentally scolding herself, Greer settled on the third step, folded open the foil covering on her dinner, and tucked her white robe around her legs. She was just putting the first bite of lasagna into her mouth when the front door flew open. Her fork stayed suspended in mid-air.

The man was a rapid blur of yellow hard hat and short sleeves and grocery bag. Greer caught only a quick glimpse of tanned square face and blue eyes before he turned rapidly. Unfortunately, Truce chose that instant to leap at him from the steps. The stranger couldn't see over his grocery bag, and the next thing Greer knew, an orange had settled on her lap, a head of lettuce was sitting next to her, the hard hat was on its last bounce at the door, and a most irritated man was draped half on her legs, half on the stairs.

"Good Lord. Are you all right?" Greer exclaimed.

Very blue, very furious eyes squinted dazedly in her direction. "Is that your cat?"

There was a time and a place for honesty. This really didn't seem to be it. Declining to answer, Greer lowered her eyes, rapidly set down her lasagna, and scrambled to pick up the lettuce and orange. "I'll take care of all this. Are you hurt?"

"No." He spat out the word with all the friendliness of a guard dog.

He was definitely irritated, but Greer didn't mind. Even hostile company was welcome after one of her phone calls. And she was honestly fascinated by refilling the man's grocery bag. People revealed so much about themselves by what they bought at the grocery store. This man was clearly a bachelor who was going to die soon of malnutrition. Oranges, lettuce, beer, three containers of cashews, apples, and two packages of Oreos. The Oreos were the worse for wear after their tumble. "I'll replace these," she said seriously as she turned back to him.

"Just . . ." He grabbed the bag from her and set it safely next to the apartment door opposite Greer's. Out of harm's way, said his body language.

Her lips twitched. "Honestly, I'm sorry," she said gravely.

"You usually eat your dinner sitting on the stairs in the hall?" he growled.

"Not . . . exactly."

"You just happened to pick tonight."

"Not . . . exactly."

"And Battle Cat—is it *exactly* yours?"

"Truce?" Greer glanced down at the feline who was winding in and around her bare legs. "You have to be kidding. I've never seen that animal before in my life."

He was silent for a minute, and when Greer peeked she could see a grin sneaking up on the corners of his mouth. And he was staring at her. Leaning back against the opposite wall, the stranger was clearly catching his breath, but at the same time his eyes were busy wandering over her legs—which she instantly tucked together—and then at the sexy hint of chartreuse satin slip—which she hurried buried under the lapels of her robe.

Her attempts to hide her figure were by long habit quick; the stranger's eyes were quicker. They settled on her oval face, the frame of bouncing nut-brown hair, the straight nose with three freckles, the untannable cream of her complexion, and her eyes—and by the time his eyes met hers, she had the sudden inexplicable urge to fidget.

It wasn't wearing only a robe that bothered her, or even that he checked out her figure. Men inevitably checked out her curves on first meeting, but few, *very* few, spent more time looking at her face. Regardless, fidgeting wasn't her thing. Sensibly, Greer plopped back down on the step and picked up her fork and TV dinner.

"I take it you're my neighbor—unless you regularly wander through strange apartment buildings finding halls to eat your dinner in?" There was an ultrapatient quality in his low-pitched voice, as if he'd already resigned himself to sharing the building with a kook.

"You should never sign a lease until you know the people you're going to live across from," Greer said gravely. "Anyway, it's not the way it looks."

"No?"

"No. It's the crank calls. Not that my reaction to them is in any way rational. I admit that my behavior is ridiculous." Greer forked in another small mouthful of lasagna. "Can't help it, though," she admitted. "In the beginning, it wasn't so bad. Actually, I thought it was kind of funny. He was nice. Honestly. I mean, he never called in the middle of the night, and one time when I told him I had company, he laid off for three days—"

"Wait a minute." Her stranger took a breath and then sank down on the top step, lazily stretching out long, denim-clad legs as if resting up for a siege. "Go on," he said politely and cleared his throat. "I must have missed the transition. Like the whole relationship between eating dinner in a hallway and receiving crank calls. Never mind. You were telling me that your obscene caller didn't phone for a few days?"

"He isn't an *obscene* caller. He's just a breather."

"I see."

"Which is why it's so ridiculous to get upset. He doesn't say or do anything terrible. And I thought I'd get rid of him when I had my telephone number changed, but no such luck. Anyway, I would hardly have been out here in the hall if I'd thought anyone was going to be around." Greer dropped her fork, rubbed her palm on the thigh of her robe, and whipped out her hand with a determinedly friendly smile. "Greer here. Mostly because my mother was a frustrated actress. Lothrup's the last name. And you're . . . ?"

"Becoming rapidly exhausted," he said flatly. His palm enclosed hers. His hand was very warm, very callused, and he withdrew it very, very quickly.

Greer repressed a smile. The fury had clearly left his eyes, and a deliciously wicked twinkle had replaced it. Well. An exasperated twinkle perhaps, but there was humor in there somewhere. "I really am a very good neighbor," she assured him gravely. "You can ask the guys upstairs. I mean, your business is your business. I pick up mail and water plants when people are on vacation. Deliver chicken soup when someone has a cold. Generally keep the cat I've never seen in my life out of sight. In a pinch, I'm not opposed to sewing on a button. Not to imply that men aren't fully capable . . ."

She had to stop for breath, which was probably just as well since she seemed to be chattering like a nervous mynah bird. Most people found Greer reserved on first meeting. But then, most people didn't meet her after one of her confrontations with The Breather. And whether the stranger meant to or not, he was winning an awful lot of brownie points by keeping his attention above her neck while they talked.

There was a dance of amusement in his eyes as he motioned for her to continue eating. "I get the message," he said gravely, "but somehow I have trouble picturing you in the role of resident housemother."

Wrong, sweetie, Greer thought with amusement. Other men had made the same mistake, and Greer had no doubts she could set her new neighbor straight in time. Figure or no figure, the femme fatale role just wasn't her scene.

Eye shadow looked clownish on her; she wasn't about to mask her freckles with makeup; and over the years she'd learned that even the most ruthless predators didn't make passes at mother figures. The defense mechanism had evolved naturally. Greer liked taking care of people, and that included men.

Since the stranger refused to stop studying her, Greer responded in kind. People-watching was one of her favorite pastimes anyway.

As handsome went, he wasn't particularly. His hair was sort of cinnamon brown, crisply curling and healthy looking. The sun had baked his skin to a warm gold. A small mustache trailed the shape of his smooth upper lip; he had a square chin and clean, strong features. Nice-looking but not outstanding. His eyes, though, were wonderfully unusual, an absolutely brilliant blue, keen and intelligent, full of life.

He didn't give all that much away with his facial expressions, but his body language said a great deal. His blue work shirt fit snugly over a broad chest, and his jeans hugged the long, smooth muscles of his thighs. His shirt was open at the throat, and a worn leather belt settled on his lean hips. The message wasn't rough-and-tough machismo, but a certain bold sexuality came with the man.

Again, Greer guessed that he was single. No self-respecting wife would have let him loose with that tiny hole in his worn jeans—not *that* high on the thigh. Assuming from his northern accent that he was new in town, Greer doubted that he'd have any problem finding female companionship in North Carolina. Even his lazy smile carried a teasing hint of sexuality.

Fine by her. On one level, certain wary instincts automatically kicked into operation when she was near a certain kind of man. On another level, Greer had erected well-entrenched defenses against her own susceptibility. Other women would see the sexuality of the lean and hungry figure. Greer's only concern was that he looked slightly underfed. She swallowed a bite of lasagna. "What do you do?" she asked curiously.

"Pardon?"

"Your work?"

"Engineer. A mechanical engineer—I spend most of my day out in the field, as you can see." He motioned to his dusty work boots. "Laughlin's the company; they're busy moving into Greenville at the moment. If the building ever *does* get done, I hope to have a little time to put up a house. I've rented this apartment for six months, but I hope to move into my own place before then. You?"

"Um." She swallowed the last morsel of food, feeling just slightly unnerved by his lazy stare. Old defenses were slipping, as he kept his eyes on her face, but she knew darn well she didn't have *that* fascinating a nose. "I work for Love Lace. Lingerie." Greer looked him straight in the eye, administering a little private test of her own.

"Doing . . . ?"

Greer set aside the aluminum tray and twined her hands loosely around her knees, relaxing. He'd passed her tiny test by not indulging in sexual innuendo about her job. "I'm their ad psychologist. If you've never heard of that job before, it's probably because my boss invented it. Grant hired me—directly out of college with an extremely useless degree in psych—to keep the marketing and design staff from killing each other. Since his wife's our head designer, he had a vested interest in her survival."

"I can understand that."

"I'm glad you can. I don't always. Basically, the lingerie industry's gone boom; Grant wants to stay in for the count, and he needed an impartial woman's viewpoint to back up his own business expertise. His wife wants to make French panties; the marketing staff says Jockey-type shorts for women are in. Somebody's got to study the public to psyche out what they really want to buy. For instance, a man can stare at a *Playboy* spread of a woman in a satin G-string, but as to whether or not he'll actually buy one for his wife— What's wrong?" Greer asked cheerfully.

"Nothing." He was choking mildly.

And Greer knew exactly what was wrong. A big ego wasn't her problem, and he'd given her no reason to think he was going to come on to her. She'd just wanted to make sure that didn't happen, and nothing took the predatory gleam out of a man's eyes quicker than an encounter with a commonsense woman who talked about unmentionables the way other people talked about toothpaste.

"You didn't mention your name," she said lightly, once he'd recovered.

"Ryan McCullough."

The name suited him. McCullough had the flavor of Scottish highlands and fresh air and the wild, rocky seacoast. And he had the look of a man who would seek out man-against-environment-type challenges. The stereotype of the plodding engineer didn't fit him at all, arousing her curiosity.

Greer kept her eyes carefully averted from his work boots, praying he wouldn't notice that Truce had settled at his feet and was trying to pull out the shoelaces. "You're from . . . ?"

"Maine, originally." He added abruptly, "How long have you been getting those phone calls?"

"Too long, but honestly, they're nothing to worry about." Greer glanced at her watch, hardly believing that nearly an hour had passed. Unfortunately, anxiety attacks always made her gregarious, but that choked-up irrational fear was gone now. Long gone, thanks to one Ryan McCullough, and she'd certainly been bending his ear long enough. She stood up and stretched. "If I'd known you were moving in, I would have brought over a dinner. As it is, tonight was rather slim pickings—"

The phone rang in her apartment, a distant jangle through walls and closed doors. Greer pivoted toward the sound, color draining from her face. Her friendly chatter ceased instantly, sliced off rapidly as if with a knife blade. When the phone rang again, her fingers curled helplessly at her sides.

Firm hands suddenly closed on her upper arms from behind. "Dammit. Now, how the hell often *does* that happen?"

Her fingers fluttered in the air. She held her breath when the phone rang a third time. Ryan's firm hands released her shoulders; he swept in front of her toward the door. "Where's your phone?" he demanded brusquely.

"Pardon?" Tiny pinpricks of moisture beaded on her forehead. She stared wildly at Ryan as the phone jangled a fourth time. Fear was the strangest emotion. A stupid, stupid emotion. There'd been no threat of harm from the heavy breather. It was all in her head, this insidious growing fear of the stranger out there in the city watching her, a man who always seemed to know when she was alone, a man who'd gone to a lot of trouble to learn her new unlisted number almost as soon as she'd had the old one changed. Why had he chosen her? What could she possibly have done to deserve this? What did he *want* from her?

"There isn't any reason to be frightened," she said haltingly. "I know that. It's totally ridiculous to get so upset..."

"Stay there." Ryan pushed open her door and disappeared while she stood there. The phone rang once more and then stopped. Very shortly after that, one Ryan McCullough leaned against her open doorway, one leg lazily hooked forward and a definitely determined look to his mouth that she hadn't noticed before. His eyes bored into hers and just wouldn't let go. His tone, by contrast, was almost ridiculously gentle. "Didn't you just offer me a dinner?"

"Did I? Was there"—she hesitated—"anyone on the line?"

"They'd hung up."

Greer gathered up Truce.

"Is the offer of dinner still open?"

Greer stared at him blankly, almost certain that she'd specifically *not* offered him dinner. "I...sure." She couldn't think. Distractedly, she watched him take the plate and then the cat from her arms.

When Ryan closed her apartment door after they'd entered, she noted vaguely that he locked it.

# Chapter Two

"Do you have any wine?" Ryan inquired.

"Wine," Greer echoed. She stared at him blankly until the word finally registered in her fogged brain, and then wandered toward the kitchen and crouched down by the cupboard near the stove. One Christmas, someone had given her a lovely wine rack; the lone bottle resting on its inexpensive side was dusty.

She wiped it clean, searched for a corkscrew, opened the bottle, and groped for a wineglass. Her movements were mechanical, her mind functioning at half power. Fear was an intangible thing. It hit in waves, like the ebb and flow of a tide, engulfing her one minute, releasing her the next.

If only she could put a face to The Breather or understand what she could possibly have done to make anyone so obsessively harass her . . . but she could find nothing, no clue to help her answer that *why*. She was well liked, successful in her work, had family and friends who loved her. After her divorce, she'd had a rough time, but her world was secure now. Secure, stable, normal—all were qualities she valued. And every single time the phone rang, she felt as if she'd been cut loose from her moorings, as if she were floundering with nothing to hold on to. It had to stop.

Turning, she held a glass of wine out to Ryan, but found he couldn't very well take it. Both his hands were busy filling a pan with water. "What on earth are you doing?"

"Cooking noodles for tuna casserole. You don't mind if I putter around a little in your kitchen, do you? Since you've already had your dinner?"

"I . . . no." Since he had half the ingredients already laid out on her counter, there seemed little else she could say. Her new neighbor had a slight tendency to mow down people in his way. Within seconds, she found herself sitting at the kitchen table with the wineglass in her hand. Rather bewildered, she sipped from it.

Ryan grinned. By the time she took another sip of wine, her hands had stopped trembling. Satisfied, he turned back to the stove. He hadn't eaten anything since breakfast, but he wasn't absolutely sure whether he was more hungry for dinner or for the lady in the white cotton robe.

On sight he'd liked her bubbling warmth, her easy humor, the natural confidence that was part of her. That appeal had been strengthened when she'd unconsciously run full tilt into his protective instincts. His new neighbor clearly didn't approach life via logical, rational thought patterns. If she did, she'd never have let a stranger into her kitchen. And she certainly wouldn't still be sitting in front of him in that robe.

Ryan was beginning to be very fond of that robe.

The lapels opened just slightly when she moved, revealing a shadow of satin-soft breasts and the promise of more. And earlier, when she walked in, the fabric had parted to reveal slim, long legs to midthigh, give or take the interim covering of a slip. Satin didn't hide much anyway, and the absolutely hideous color of her slip fascinated him.

Within seconds of meeting her, he'd figured out she was sensitive about that outstanding figure of hers, and she hadn't wasted any time letting him know she was the girl-next-door kind of neighbor, not fair game.

Fine. Both men and women transmitted sexual available-or-not signals on first meeting. Greer's choice of signals intrigued him. The neon-colored slip, the motherly neighbor routine, her matter-of-fact mention of Jockey shorts: The message was a blunt *Don't waste your time; this lady's only interest in bed is sleeping.*

The message was interesting.

Particularly since she was the sexiest lady he'd come across in a long time.

Her figure stirred definite temptations, but not exclusively. At thirty-four, Ryan was too old to believe that the allure of a potential lover lay solely in her curves and dimensions. Sleeping partners came in all shapes. The best of lovers brought much more to bed than flesh and bones. And it was Greer's face that radiated all the promise in the word *lover*.

Her voice came from deep in her throat, as lazy and sensual as black silk. Her dark, soft eyes and other features were not quite beautiful, yet they were mobile, expressive, feminine. Her hair was brown with sun streaks, the style short and casual, wind-tossed and touchable. That was it, exactly. All of her looked infinitely touchable. She radiated vibrance, a graceful energy, a woman's special joy in life.

He couldn't shake the desire to see her naked, to touch and taste, to see if she was as special as his instincts told him she was.

He glanced fleetingly around the kitchen. Hanging plants were clustered in front of the windows; embroidered pictures hung everywhere. The chair seats were needlepoint, and recipes had been jammed into thick cookbooks on the counter. The walls had been painted a warm, feminine coral, and an overstuffed purse perched on a chair near the door. It was a baking-bread kind of kitchen, as no doubt the lady meant it to be. More unambiguous messages that the lady was a homebody rather than a lustful lover.

Perhaps.

Ryan stirred his concoction on the stove. "Almost ready for another glass of wine?"

"Pardon?" It was certainly past time to stop mulling over her mysterious caller. Greer glanced ruefully down at her empty wineglass. "I believe this was intended for you."

"Maybe later." He'd itched to hold her when she'd been so upset, but she'd hardly known him an hour. The wine, at least, had calmed her down, and there was color in her face again. Sinking into the chair across from her, Ryan reached for his plate and the wine bottle. "I seem to have made enough food for two, and I'll refill your glass . . ."

"No, thanks. Really." She'd regained her emotional equilibrium, watching him cook. Actually, what she'd really regained was her sense of humor. He was certainly aggressive about finding the pans, but his knowledge of what to do with them afterward was not so extensive. With her chin perched on her palm, Greer peered at his culinary effort, a sassy grin on her mouth. "Are you absolutely positive that's edible?"

"I'll have you know I survived through college on tuna-noodle casserole."

"'Surviving' looks like the applicable word," Greer teased.

"Now, don't judge until you've tasted." He speared a small amount on a fork and aimed it at her mouth.

Their eyes met for a fraction of an instant before her lips enclosed the morsel. His were very blue, very warm, and oddly intimate. No man had looked at Greer like that in a very long time.

She swallowed hurriedly, having to remember to taste the bite on the way down. "Have you considered buying a basic cookbook?" she asked sympathetically. "There are some good ones that even beginners can cope with."

Ryan sighed. "There's nothing more annoying than a chauvinistic woman," he mentioned to the ceiling.

"Hey. That wasn't a sexist comment." Greer paused. "Although if you *had* lived in caveman times, I think you'd have done better waving your club around and looking cool while you invented the wheel than fussing around the old cooking fire. I don't want to imply that mankind would have totally died out from this recipe, but..."

"I've tickled my sisters half to death for far less offensive insults than that," Ryan informed her.

Greer chuckled even as she felt a slight wariness at the reference to tickling. "Luckily, I've never had that particular sensitivity," she said smoothly. "Even my little toes aren't ticklish—and heaven knows, my older sister used to try."

Ryan received and acknowledged the tiny warn-off signal. He couldn't help it if he still wanted her alone for an hour on a king-sized mattress in order to check out her ticklishness personally.

"Are you going to tell me about your crank calls?" he asked abruptly.

"Sure. If you want to hear."

"I want to hear." He didn't want to upset her again by making her talk about it, but she had no choice. Whether or not she appreciated the interference, he wasn't about to go across the hall and unpack without first getting answers to a few questions. "Exactly how long have you been getting the calls? When did they start? Have you called the police? The phone company?"

Greer smiled and reached over to pat his arm reassuringly. "Why am I getting the impression you think I haven't handled the problem?" she asked wryly. "Now, I know I made a bad first impression, but I'm twenty-seven years old and have been managing my own life for some time now. *Of course* I've called the police and phone company."

"And?"

"And nothing. The police were nice, but they take action only if the caller's potentially dangerous. Mine's a mere breather. They tactfully referred me to the phone company, which puts breathers in the nuisance category. Nuisance calls just aren't worth the same attention as abusive or obscene calls."

"So they haven't done anything." Ryan's eyes darkened.

"They've done lots. They changed my number and gave me piles of forms to fill out. For a couple of weeks they even put a tracer on my phone; *and* they're extremely sympathetic. But it *is* silly to get upset, you know. Crank callers, I gather, are like flashers. They get a perverse thrill out of upsetting women, but no one's getting physically threatened or hurt."

"Honey..." Ryan started irritably. She'd done her share; he heard that. He'd never had anyone hand him a problem that didn't have a solution. Mountains were probably put there to climb. And where he grew up, a man didn't abandon a woman who was seriously afraid and simply hand her some *forms*.

In the living room, the telephone barely trilled before Ryan leaped out of his chair and lurched for it. Before Greer had the chance to get nervous, he was barking her name from the other room.

"Someone named Daniel," he growled as he handed her the receiver.

"Dan?" she said. "No, that was my new neighbor." With the receiver cupped to her ear, Greer smiled into Ryan's blue eyes, a little startled to see that the dance in them had been replaced by little chips of ice. "Sure, Friday night will be fine..." No problem, she mouthed to Ryan, the caller was a friend.

He stuffed his hands loosely into his jeans pockets, but hovered until she hung up the telephone. After that, he took on the dishes while she made coffee.

An hour later, she was curled in the old wicker rocker, and Ryan, in his stocking feet, was stretched out on the couch. Tuesday evenings were usually a boring midpoint in the week, but not this one. Greer couldn't remember feeling as at ease and content in anyone's company on first meeting.

He was from Maine, he told her, a simple old-fashioned backwoods town not far from the Atlantic coast.

He clearly loved the place. Unfortunately, the town offered limited opportunities for a mechanical engineer; he'd worked for six years for one company, but there'd been no hope of further advancement. He was interested in starting his own firm eventually, but he didn't have the varied experience he needed to do that just yet—and Laughlin had snapped him up after seeing his qualifications, grateful that he was willing to move to North Carolina.

Of the women in his life he said nothing, Greer noted, but the longer she listened to him, the more she was conscious that first impressions were deceiving. His looks weren't ordinary at all. His eyes often sparkled with fine dry humor; he had an endearing crooked grin; and his body . . . there was something about that body that reminded her of lumberjacks or shipbuilders. Energy, vitality, the lithe way he moved . . . he was so clearly a physical man.

For an instant, she could picture him being *very* physical. A slim, svelte blonde popped into Greer's imagination. A very sexy lady. A totally naked lady. She suited him very well, Greer mused. In a lover, he would clearly want a physically expressive woman, an uninhibited mate, a boldly sexual match for his own—

Abruptly, she swallowed, feeling a faint heat climb up her cheeks. *Behave yourself, Greer.* She always analyzed people on first meeting, but she rarely fantasized about their sex lives.

". . . enemies?"

Greer blinked awake and rapidly reached for the half-full coffee cup on the table next to her. "Pardon?"

"Have you thought about who might be making those calls to you? What about this *Daniel,* for instance?"

She had no interest in returning to the upsetting topic

of The Breather, but Ryan's question made her smile. "Daniel wouldn't swat a mosquito on his brave days. I've known him for several months; he's a very brilliant accountant, but he's unbelievably shy."

Ryan gave a private snort. *Shy* was the easiest game in town to pull off for a man on the make; it immediately aroused a woman's protective urges.

And a woman's special vulnerabilities immediately aroused a man's protective urges. He was having a bad case of that problem, looking at her. Greer was curled up in the chair like a kitten. Barefoot, her hair softly ruffled, her skin clear and smooth and without makeup, a sleepy, vulnerable look in her eyes ... she would look very much like that after she'd just made love. His libido stirred restlessly. Moments before, he'd been certain she'd been thinking of a man, and he'd felt a sharp, unexpected surge of jealousy.

"If you're sure it isn't Daniel ... there must be other men?" he questioned casually.

"Enemies? I have tons of enemies," Greer said wryly. "I've thought about Steve McManus for one—he's the guy I stole the cat from."

"I beg your pardon?"

"He lived two buildings down the street, left the cat alone for weeks at a time. He knows I took Truce because I left him a note."

Ryan cleared his throat. "Perhaps you could come up with a more dangerous enemy than that."

"Now, just because you don't like cats—"

"It *did* occur to me that McManus might have been grateful." Ryan raised his hands defensively at Greer's look of mock outrage. "Sorry. Of course you're right. He must hate you for life for stealing his cat, but in the meantime ..."

Greer paused thoughtfully. "Well. There's John. My ex-husband," she explained. "I couldn't really call him an enemy, but he wasn't very happy over the divorce."

"John," Ryan echoed irritably. There had to be a reason why he'd never liked that name. "How long have you been divorced?"

"Four years. I still see him on occasion, though."

"You were married for a long time?"

His questions would have struck her as prying if he weren't so obviously investigating her crank calls. For months, Greer had worried in private as to who her caller might be. She'd never discussed the problem with her family because she hadn't wanted to worry them. Ryan was a stranger, but he was also clearly a rational, objective man. And as long as he was willing to listen...

"John and I were married for two years," Greer admitted hesitantly, and then started talking in a rush, anxious to hear Ryan's opinion when he understood the relationship. "The thing was, like most psychology majors fresh out of college, I was very good at taking on the misunderstood, the unwanted, the lost souls. John was one of those. Rotten childhood, parents who didn't care..." Greer bit her lip absently and gave Ryan a small smile. "I was very sure that an understanding woman was all he needed to turn his life around. Only two years later, I wasn't quite so fresh out of college. Perhaps he *was* a lost soul, but he was also incurably lazy. And very happy to be taken care of full time in high style." She added wearily, "I was still paying off his debts two years after the divorce. It wasn't the best of times."

"You think he would call you now—just to harass you?"

"No. But you asked about enemies. I'm trying to give you my best list," Greer said wryly, then snapped her fingers. "I forgot about Andrew."

"Who the he—on earth is *Andrew?*"

Greer's eyebrows shot up in amusement at the way
Ryan's fingers were suddenly drumming a tattoo on the
couch. "My brother-in-law," she answered mildly. "My
sister died six years ago in a traffic accident. Their daughter Robin is ten now and a confirmed runaway. Andrew
isn't a bad father, but he's busy, and Robin's a little witch
at finding clever ways to get his attention. Her favorite
trick is to pack a suitcase and cart it across town to me."

"To you," Ryan echoed.

Greer nodded. "Andrew always knows where she is,
but he does get upset, and we've had a few words now
and then. I probably *do* cater to Robin too much, but if
he'd give her more of his time . . . she *needs* his attention." Greer's eyes took on a fierce, protective light, then
faded. "Anyway, he's not too fond of me, but still. In
terms of the identity of my breather, I really don't think . . ."

Neither did Ryan. Strays cats, stray men, stray children, he thought dismally. Quite a hit list. He glanced
down to where the cat had leaped on his stomach and
was kneading his shirt, staring up at him with limpid
eyes. "You work more with men or women?" he questioned abruptly.

"More with men, I suppose. That must sound strange
in the lingerie industry, but it isn't, really. It's a business
like any other business. Anyway, I've worked with everyone there for years."

Ryan fell silent, pensively stroking the cat until the
feline raised his chin with a rumbling purr and Ryan
realized what he was doing. His hand dropped abruptly,
and he shot Greer a deadpan stare. "You've got one hell
of a list of enemies, Greer. Sounds to me like you need
a permanent bodyguard."

Greer chuckled, feeling immediate and inexplicable relief. She'd never wanted to believe that either Andrew or John was her caller, but they were the closest she had to suspicious characters in her life. "There's also the man I beat in a chess tournament in college—"

"God. The hate list is *still* going on?"

"And I bumped a guy's fender when I was sixteen."

"Finally, someone with cause," Ryan said dryly, and Greer chuckled again. "How about the other men in your life besides this Daniel?" he asked matter-of-factly.

Greer stretched, weary from sitting still for so long. "I go out with a few others, but no one who would do anything like that."

Ryan made a small sound.

"What's wrong?" she asked immediately.

"Nothing. I was just thinking . . ."

"What?" Greer leaned forward intently.

"I don't want to offend you by being too personal . . ."

"You won't," she assured him.

"Well. Daniel and your other men friends are probably very nice. I'm *sure* they are, so don't misunderstand. But if you don't know them extremely well . . ." He let his voice trail off. Greer said nothing. Ryan cleared his throat. "You're sure you know them *extremely* well?" he asked gravely.

"Well. Hardly their deepest secrets, if that's what you mean," Greer answered thoughtfully. "Even so, I'm a long way from a naive high school girl as far as judging character goes. Really, I can't picture any of them making those calls."

Fine. He still didn't know whether she was sleeping with anyone on a regular basis, but Ryan had no right to pursue that subject.

They talked a little longer before he restlessly stood

up, apologizing for taking up so much of her evening.

Greer just shook her head, trailing him to the door.
"You were awfully kind, listening to me for an entire
evening. As a little kid, I wasn't afraid of the goblins in
the night, but I have to admit that lately I've been nervous
staying alone."

The thought grew as they reached the door. It was
because Ryan had been there that she hadn't felt nervous.
He was a very comforting, understanding, strong kind
of man to have as a neighbor. He'd made her feel safer
than she'd felt in months. Impulsively, she touched his
hand as he pulled open the door. He turned, a question
in his eyes.

She stood on tiptoe and swung her arms around his
neck in a quick hug. Affection came as naturally to her
as breathing, and there was no question that Ryan was
a huggable man. She clung to the warmth of his body,
more grateful than she could tell him for laying her ghosts
to rest that evening. "Thank you again," she said simply.
"And I promise I won't talk your ear off the next time
I see you. I'm hardly in the habit of laying problems on
a stranger's doorstep, honest."

She smiled, expecting to see his own easy smile in
return.

He didn't smile back. She wasn't exactly sure what
happened. One minute she was smiling affectionately up
at him and her arms were slipping down from his shoulders. In the next, he'd captured her arms and his smooth,
warm mouth descended on hers with a pressure that was
starkly, boldly sexual. All heat, all fire, all such a startling
surprise of warm-blooded male . . . She didn't pull back;
she was too shocked.

Not angry, not distressed. Just shocked. In seconds,
he'd realize that she wasn't responding: This was no

teenage boy but a man. And Greer was no longer a
frightened girl but a woman who never responded until
time and gentleness and trust had won her over. Blunt
sexuality no longer frightened her; it simply turned her
off.

Only this time something strange was happening.
Ryan's tongue was playing on the seam of her lips, forcing them to part. That smooth, warm tongue slipped
inside, touching hers. She could feel the strength of his
arms holding her, the warmth of him, an alien rush of
. . . foolish sensations. He wasn't waiting for a response.
He was expecting it, demanding it. And that something
strange kept happening, because that sensual rush kept
coming, and like a candle, she wanted to burn and melt.

Ryan's lips rose from hers abruptly. Brusquely, with
a trace of roughness, he changed from lover to brother.
He tugged the lapels of her robe together and ran a quick
hand through her hair as if he were suddenly determined
to obliterate the sensual toss of her hair. The kiss might
never have been, except that the look in his eyes was
fierce, bright, and stark with wanting. "You *do* need a
bodyguard," he said gruffly.

"I . . . Pardon?"

"Lock your door and keep it locked. *Now,* Greer."

He was gone.

Greer was left bewildered and mildly irritated. Exactly
what had *happened?* Surely he hadn't changed from Jekyll to Hyde simply because she'd demonstrated a little
basic human affection?

She glanced at the gold-framed mirror in the hall and
saw a woman with tousled hair and no makeup, wearing
a threadbare robe. Ryan didn't strike her as a man who
would ever be *that* desperate.

Men just didn't jump her, not anymore. A long time

ago, Greer had had enough of being wanted for her body, and she knew better than to send out any "available" signals until she knew a man well. She *knew* she hadn't sent them out to Ryan, not because she didn't immediately like him, but because she simply didn't know him well enough.

For whatever reasons that kiss had happened, it left her unsettled the rest of the night.

# Chapter Three

WEARING A PASTEL green suit and matching sandals, Greer was perched on the conference table, her legs swinging as she waited for the discussion to die down.

The conference room, like the offices at Love Lace, was thickly carpeted in pale pink. Flocked ivory wallpaper added an elegant touch; the paperweights were mother-of-pearl; and the ambience from the sewing room to the customer entrance was supposed to reflect luxurious serenity—an atmosphere conducive to the selling of lingerie.

Greer had known for a long time that the atmosphere was a scam. Marketing panties was as cutthroat as any other business, if not more so. Greer's glasses were perched on her nose as she surveyed the three pairs of male eyes glaring stubbornly at her.

"You all appear to be deaf this morning," she said cheerfully. "I agree that the nightgown is a unique design—one of the sexiest we've ever had. It just won't do at all for the catalog cover."

"The hell it won't," growled the tall blond in front. Barney tossed copies of designs on the table in front of him. "The others don't hold a candle to it, Greer. And since you're the only holdout—"

"And Marie's vote would be on our side. You know that," Tim interrupted.

Greer nodded patiently. The two potential choices for their fall catalog cover design were lying next to her. One was a pastel yellow lounging outfit, an infinitely soft design that draped loosely over the model's figure. The look was sensual, comfortable, and subtly alluring.

That was the one the men didn't like. Their favorite was Marie's coup de grâce, a negligee in pearl-pink satin and cream lace. The model wearing it had a *Penthouse* figure—which the gown required. Satin, however luxurious, was not an easy fabric for most women to wear. It had a sheen and, like a mirror, reflected a woman's worst faults. The gown flowed over a body that had to be perfect, from flat stomach to smooth hips and long legs. The cobweb-lace bodice cupped breasts that had to be sizable and tilted up just so. The low, heart-shaped neckline, the cutouts showing the sides of the breasts— only a certain kind of woman could wear the style, a sexually uninhibited woman who had the courage to flaunt her assets.

"If our customers were men, I would agree with you," Greer continued patiently. "But they're women. Women we want as return customers."

"Women who are increasingly buying sexy lingerie,

or we wouldn't all be here now," Ray drawled from the chair closest to her. "Sex is in this decade, sweetheart. We're asking you to catch up and become part of the times..."

Greer tossed a wad of paper in his general direction. Grant, from the back of the room, didn't so much as raise an eyelid. "You can sell the nightgown on that basis," Greer said evenly. "And it *will* sell, even if the price is much higher than for our usual lingerie. You're still missing the point. The nightgown doesn't enhance the image we want Love Lace to project, and in the long run, we'd lose money because of it."

The argument raged on. Greer's eyes darted back and forth between the men in front of her, her tone calm and her stance never wavering. This morning the men were generally behaving like turkeys. Normally, she was pretty fond of them.

In front of her sat Barney. In his mid-thirties, Barney was tall and blond and divorced. His specialty was fabric and tech care; he was great at his job, but she'd had a few problems with his roving hands when she first started working at Love Lace. There'd been no passes, however, after he'd had the flu and she'd taken chicken soup to his home... and listened for six hours to his divorce woes.

Tim, on the other side of the table, was the firm's accountant. He looked harmless enough with his fluff of gray hair and myopic brown eyes, but he was one of the most confirmed misogynists Greer had ever met... until she'd discovered he was a sucker for doughnuts in the morning. The way to *some* men's hearts was still through their stomachs.

In the back of the room sat Grant, the boss, a small, spare man with thinning hair, a wisp of a mustache, a gentle voice, and the business instincts of a shark. Throughout the meeting, his face remained expressionless, except for the faintest of smiles as he watched his ad psychologist in action.

One of Grant's favorite management strategies was never to conduct a staff meeting himself. Actually, few of his business methods followed a standard set of rules— they just worked, and woe to any competitor who misjudged his gentle look as weakness. Greer thought affectionately that the man had only one major flaw: He couldn't stand arguing with his French wife.

Today he didn't have to, because Marie had stayed home with a cold. Volatile and brilliantly creative, Marie was their chief designer. On the rare occasions when Grant didn't feel that one of his wife's designs would sell, he expected Greer to be his hatchet woman. And the cream lace on pink satin was Marie's choice for their fall catalog cover, or someone's life was going to be miserable.

Probably Greer's, though she doubted Grant would escape the flying shrapnel when his wife returned to work.

Regardless, Grant had warned her when she started with Love Lace that there were areas in which she'd have to sink or swim. Because of her looks, she was better prepared than some to deal with sexism. She'd managed Barney and Tim, but Ray was her last holdout, and it was Ray who followed her to her office once the staff meeting was over.

He paused in the doorway while she tossed her glasses on her desk and unloaded the mound of paperwork in her arms. "You won again," he remarked idly.

"Hmmm." Greer scanned the messages next to the phone before glancing up. Ray was their resident feudal baron, she thought whimsically. Black hair, black eyes, a subtle smile, broad shoulders in meticulous dress: He only needed a castle with moat to complete the picture. And an estate populated by women who bowed to him.

Ray could market oceanfront property in Kansas successfully, and Greer respected him for that. But at times his salesmanship didn't make him any easier to work with. Ray generally backed down just before a clash, but he and Greer inevitably circled each other in conversation like wary combatants.

Leaning against her office door, he lazily crossed his ankles. "Marie will have your hide."

"You're telling me something I don't know?"

Ray chuckled and moved in to slouch comfortably in the pale gray chair next to her desk. "It *would* have made a good cover."

"For Frederick's of Hollywood." Greer sat down and slipped off her shoes. The others were used to her padding around in stocking feet; she wasn't about to change her habits for Ray. As she waited for him to speak, she was aware that his eyes were roving over her mint-green suit, slowly removing that suit, and just as slowly continuing to talk with her stark naked—in his imagination. Used to his mode of operation, she paid little attention.

"You're one of the few women who could wear that nightgown to absolute perfection," Ray drawled.

"Yup," Greer agreed smoothly. "Unfortunately, pink makes my face break out in spots."

Annoyance flamed in his dark eyes, but only for an instant before he let out a low chuckle. "I still think I caught just a glint of lust in your eyes when you looked at that nightgown. Don't tell me we've found a rare weakness in you, Greer?"

Something sharp pricked her finger, and she glanced

down in surprise. The paper clip in her hand was completely bent out of shape, unusable now. Had she really just done that? Tossing the thing in the wastebasket, she let her eyes return to Ray. "I know you're ticked because you were backing Marie on this one, but rationally you know better. Cost margins were part of it—the nightgown is too much higher than our regular lines. And style is part of it—the style simply has limited appeal; too few women would look good in it."

"You want me to listen to your whole lecture again?" he asked dryly.

Greer leaned forward, resting her chin in her cupped hands, wondering why *some* men remained uneducable. "We're selling fantasies," she said patiently. "The whole business of lingerie is based on people's fondness for make-believe. We sell sinfully delicious fantasies—daydreams that don't threaten. A woman is going to buy what makes her feel good about herself. What feels good next to her skin. Clothes that give her confidence because she *does* feel sexy in them. And that's entirely different from a nightgown that shouts—"

"Sex object. 'Promoting sexuality is inherent to the field, but it doesn't have to be on a sex-object basis'," Ray quoted with another of his subtle smiles, mimicking her earlier words in the staff meeting. "One of the staff can be very, very picky on that infinitesimal difference between sexy and sex object."

"A *huge* difference," Greer corrected.

"You're full of peanuts, darling."

*Control your temper, Greer.* "You voted with me in the end," she reminded him.

"That was business. Business is a different game from life." He stood up and stretched lazily, his opaque, hypnotic eye fastened on her. "I really only came in to say

I was shocked you didn't have a little feminine temper tantrum over going with me to the trade show."

"Why on earth should I?"

He shrugged. "You've backed out of attending every other trade show before this."

It was true—she *had*. Because lingerie conventions were just like other conventions. A lone woman was a prize lamb in a meat market, something Greer would never willingly let herself in for. And the minute she'd yielded to Grant's suggestion at the end of the staff meeting that she go, she knew Ray would offer a suggestive comment. "Love Lace always sends two representatives," she said smoothly, "and since Marie can't go with you this time, I don't mind."

"Somehow I thought you would."

"Why?"

"You and I rather rub each other the wrong way, don't we? On the other hand, we could probably solve that rather quickly if we took a double room at the convention."

Greer frowned innocently, as if considering. "Sex does solve *everything*," she said cheerfully, "but I doubt it would work in this instance. I snore—loudly, I'm told. You'd get crabby from lack of sleep, and then we'd never stop bickering."

"I didn't have in mind getting all that much sleep, anyway."

"Would you kindly get your bedroom eyes out of here so I can get some work done?"

Ray chuckled, pausing only for another second at the door. "Are you that sassy with the men in your life, Greer?"

"Worse," she said absently, and deliberately opened a folder on her desk. He was gone a few seconds later.

Her pulse slowed down a few moments afterward. Ray inevitably ruffled the figurative fur on the back of her neck. She didn't know why she let him do it. There was a psychological label for men who didn't feel sexually secure about themselves unless they were aggressive with the females of the species. Whatever the term, it was her own problem that she let him continue to bother her.

She worked for an hour and accomplished precisely nothing. When the clock struck twelve, she put on her shoes, grabbed her purse, and sauntered to the front door.

On the street, a soft breeze fluttered through the leaves in restless surges. The day was warm, bright with the North Carolina sun. Settling her sunglasses on her nose, she slid her hands into the pockets of her suit and simply strolled, taking in the springtime mood and relaxing.

The offices near Love Lace were well landscaped; gay rows of colorful flowers danced in the faint breeze, neat and confined within their borders and as new as the season. The smell of freshly mown grass filled her nostrils, and birds were rocking on the branches overhead, most of them in pairs. Another sign of spring.

The sun's touch on her face felt as sensual as a caress. Her mood half lazy, half oddly wistful, Greer strolled through the business district and window-shopped. She paused before a display showing a rose-colored evening gown, and thought helplessly of the pink satin negligee. The damn thing, she was well aware, was starting to haunt her, but *not* because she hadn't been right about the catalog cover.

Cream lace on pink satin . . . maybe every woman had a secret fantasy about color and texture and whatever it was that made her feel sultry and sexy and exotic. That negligee was Greer's. She wasn't the type to wear it; even the thought of wearing it raised a fleeting feeling of nameless anxiety, but she couldn't get the thing out of her mind.

She hadn't been able to get her new neighbor out of her mind, either. She'd woken up thinking about Ryan, and at most inconvenient times all morning she hadn't been able to get him out of her head.

His kiss bothered her. The men who knew her would never have misunderstood a simple gesture of affection; he obviously thought she'd invited that kiss with her own behavior. Because they were going to be neighbors, she obviously had to find some way to correct a misleading impression if she'd given one.

Glancing at her watch, Greer turned around and ambled back toward work, suddenly feeling restless, unsettled. Something about her new neighbor seemed to bring on a bad case of spring fever.

She'd known and worked with a lot of men in the last five years. As a girl, she'd hid her figure in oversized clothes, but that nonsense was all past. These days she had no reason to hide, and dressed to reflect the woman she was. Gentle colors and subtle styles suited her; sexy fashions didn't. She happened to be a naturally affectionate, caring woman, but *not* the type to lure out the sexual predator in a man.

Ryan—she couldn't fathom why—felt like danger.

Greer was too sensible to let a dangerous case of spring fever get her down.

*"Off* the counter if you value your life," Greer warned Truce. For once, the feline seemed to realize she meant business. He immediately leaped down and paced in wounded silence toward the living room.

Blowing a wisp of hair from her eyes, Greer turned the steaming bread out of the loaf pan and set it on a plate. Next to it was a luscious chocolate cake covered with two inches of seven-minute frosting. Licking her fingers, Greer stood back to survey her masterpieces with a critical eye.

They passed. They *definitely* passed. The loaf was tall and golden brown, and smelled . . . irresistible. And the cake—if she said so herself—would tempt the most determined weight watcher. Satisfied, Greer glanced at the clock, noted it was just after nine o'clock, and realized absently that her crank caller had actually left her alone for an entire evening. It seemed a good omen. Resolutely, she balanced the cake plate in one hand and the bread in the other.

Truce didn't make the juggling act any easier by trying to wind around her legs at the door. "I'll be right back. Promise," Greer told him.

Turning the knob was a precarious business, but she managed, and padded barefoot across the hall. Using her elbow as a knocker, she thumped on her new neighbor's door and waited.

No answer. Earlier Greer had heard various thumps and rattles through their shared apartment wall; she was certain Ryan was home. Chewing her lip indecisively, she tried her elbow on the bell and threatened the bread with a dire future if it toppled.

"Just open it," Ryan's voice finally yelled impatiently from within.

"I can't."

"You'll have to."

Hmm. Pasting an innocuously cheerful smile on her face, Greer managed to turn the knob with her wrist and push it open. "Ryan?"

Boxes and packing crates greeted her. Of course he'd only moved in a few days before, but Greer still couldn't help smiling. He had obviously unpacked assorted tools and books as a first priority, whereas he hadn't bothered with anything so mundane as putting up his bed—a queen-sized mattress was lying plop center on the living room carpet. *Men*.

"I heard that."

"I never said a thing." Greer swung around to face him—as well as she could with her arms full.

Like Greer, Ryan had tousled hair and bare feet; he was wearing jeans so old they were a soft gray-blue. But whereas Greer wore a scarf and a holey sweatshirt, Ryan was bare from the waist up.

Very bare. Strikingly bare. His chest was sun-browned; his shoulders sleek and muscular, and his jeans hung low over lean hips. Crisp, curling hair grew in an intimate line from his throat to his navel.

For an instant, Greer felt a strong, unfamiliar emotional rush, making her palms feel oddly slippery, her world tilt slightly off-balance. She tried to banish it. Certainly the rest of Ryan's appearance was enough to bring back her natural humor. He was covered with paint. Speckles of white dotted his mustache, his chest hair, and his jeans, and both hands glistened with them . . . partly because he was still holding a paintbrush.

Greer took a breath and then chuckled. "I can see why you couldn't answer your door," she said lightly. "Don't tell me you don't share Mrs. Wissler's love for purple?"

"I'm glad you came over," he said quietly. "If I'd known it was you—"

"Just bringing welcome-to-the-neighborhood offerings." Greer rushed past him, her arms beginning to give out even before she reached his kitchen counter. Sensibly, she plopped down her peace offerings, while most unreasonably her pulse was throbbing a mile a minute. She'd heard his low, vibrant baritone, the obvious glad-to-see-you here in his voice. "I didn't come to stay, just to cart over the cake and bread," she called back brightly. "I have this terrible problem when I come home from a tough day; I can't sit still and inevitably find myself in the kitchen. Then, though, there's this problem with cal-ories—which I figured I could shift on to you, being the nearest unfortunate neighbor. No hurry returning the plates—"

*You can stop jabbering any time, Greer.* She hadn't meant to stay, and she now found herself in a great hurry to leave once she'd deposited her gifts in his kitchen.

Wiping her palms on the seat of her jeans, she whirled for the doorway, and found Ryan's dark shadow blocking it. Her best company smile immediately curved her lips. "Honest, I'm not staying," she repeated.

"Did you get another phone call tonight?"

"Nope. He must be taking a vacation. Hardly ever misses a Wednesday." It was *still* easy to talk to him. The only difference was the memory of a thirty-second kiss, and a feeling of sexual awareness Greer hadn't had the day before.

She tried to shake it off, but it wasn't that simple with Ryan standing there half naked, a silent apartment behind him, and his soft, luminous eyes on hers. Had she really thought him ordinary-looking yesterday?

He wasn't at all. He had the sleek, lean look of an animal in the wild, the body of a man who used his muscles to do far more than push paper around a desk. His maleness assaulted her in the suddenly intimate si-lence, and Greer felt totally irritated with herself. It was one thing to be unnerved by a man who threatened her, but another thing altogether to get uptight when the man had done nothing but be friendly . . . give or take one kiss. "I'll be going . . ."

"Stay a minute and see what I'm doing."

She shook her head. "Really, I still have a ton of things to do."

"Just for a minute," Ryan coaxed.

"You're busy," she informed him firmly.

"And if I have to face one more purple room alone, I think I'll suffer apoplexy. Have you ever tried to outstare a dead purple wall?"

"Actually, no." Greer took a breath, and another step closer to the door. Ryan didn't move. She smiled engagingly at him. "Something told me you wouldn't keep the purple walls. Honestly, though, I don't want to get in your way."

"You don't have to pick up a paintbrush, I promise. Just spare me a few minutes of conversation."

"Really, I . . ." She'd only come to set things straight, and in Frank Sinatra fashion, her way. If she made an act of pure uncomplicated friendship, he would have to react in kind. And since she was dressed like a bag lady, she figured he'd get the rest of the message.

Maybe he was getting the rest of the message, Greer thought dismally, but for some unknown reason she seemed to be headed toward his bedroom a few seconds later.

# Chapter Four

FORTY-FIVE MINUTES later, Greer was perched on the fourth rung of a ladder with a paintbrush in her hand, doing her darndest to work up a sweat. As fast as she slathered white latex on the purple corner, she was dipping the brush back into the coffee can Ryan had given her.

"I really didn't ask you in to put you to work." From behind her, Ryan's tone was laced with amusement. "Do you always paint as though you're attacking your worst enemy?"

Greer's bare toes curled on the ladder rung, but she didn't turn her head. "When it's the purple villain, yes," she said blithely. "If I had to eat scrambled eggs in the morning staring at dark purple walls, I believe I'd be able to give up breakfast." Without turning, she added, "What are you planning on doing with the room after this, or have you decided yet?"

Ryan paused, as he dipped his roller into the paint. "Beyond getting rid of the purple, I haven't worried about it much, knowing I'll build my own place as soon as possible. I don't know ... At home, I had a corner fireplace in the bedroom—but this climate hardly calls for it. The stereo has to go in here; I almost always listen to music before sleeping..."

Or seducing, Greer thought darkly. Fireplaces, firm mattresses, and music at midnight ... it all suited him. Her paintbrush swish-swished over the wall at the speed of sound. *Why* couldn't he have needed his *kitchen* painted instead of the bedroom? Why did these silly images keep popping into her head?

Oh, well. In a half-hour, the room would be done. He'd already finished three walls and the ceiling before she came in. A little molding and one windowsill were all that remained, except for the wall Ryan was painting now. She climbed down from the ladder and started working on the windowsill.

Truthfully, she didn't mind helping him. Facing house projects after a long day's work was never any fun alone. And even though he was only a short-term resident, she wasn't surprised that he wanted a fresh coat of paint on the place—not simply because he couldn't live with Mrs. Wissler's purple, but also because he was clearly a man who'd want to put his own stamp on a place.

Her eyes darted to Ryan. His forehead was dotted with moisture, and damp brown hair curled on his brow. An evening beard darkened his chin, and Greer found herself staring at it, then letting her eyes wander deliberately down to his bare, muscled chest.

She relaxed. No dreadful rush of sexual emotions assaulted her. These little fantasies that kept cropping up in her head were absolutely ridiculous. Ryan had done little but tease her and make her laugh. There'd been nothing to make her believe he was even seriously interested. "I should have brought Truce," she said absently as she picked up the paintbrush again. "He'll be howling up a storm next door. He doesn't seem to mind if I'm gone all day, but if I leave at night I always come home to those pitiful wails."

"A cat that needs a baby-sitter," muttered Ryan.

"I take it you're a dog man."

"Was that meant as an insult?"

She shook her head, laughing. "No, but people always seem to go one way or the other. German Shepherd?" she guessed.

"Great Pyrenees. I left her with my brother in Maine. I knew there'd be no place for her to run here."

"I thought the Pyrenees were mountains."

"They're also big white dogs. Would you *stop* working like a Roman slave, please? You're hitting my masculine ego where it hurts. I can't keep up with you."

"You poor thing," Greer began, and dropped her paintbrush on the tarp at her feet when she heard the faint but unmistakable ring of a telephone through the paper-thin walls.

Behind her, she heard Ryan setting down his paint roller. "Your apartment's unlocked?"

"Yes, but don't. Really. I—"

He paused only long enough to grab a rag for his hands before he disappeared. Greer gnawed on her lip, then picked up her brush and dipped it in the paint can again. Dip and stroke, dip and stroke. Her heart was trying to condense into a tight, hard beating ball in her chest, yet Ryan couldn't have been gone five minutes.

"A man named Michael," he said briskly. "I told him you had your hands full of paint and you'd call him back when you could."

Greer took a huge breath. "Thanks. For a minute, I was afraid it was my favorite crank call—"

"So who's Michael?" Ryan interrupted conversationally. "Another potential heavy breather?"

Expecting him to pick up his roller again, Greer was startled when he blocked her from behind. He stole her paintbrush from one hand and a small rag from the other. For one very small moment, the backs of her thighs were cradled against the fronts of his, and Greer stood immobile as a statue. "No. Just someone I occasionally go out wi—what on earth are you doing?"

"Break time," Ryan announced, moving away from her.

"But we could have the whole room finished in just a few minutes..." Her voice trailed off. He'd already disappeared into the hall.

"I brought Truce with me," Ryan called over his shoulder, "so he wouldn't start howling if you stayed a few more minutes."

"Oh. Well, that was nice of you, but..." Greer let her voice trail off again, so he wouldn't hear the hint of doubt. Not that saving the cat wasn't kind, but somehow the man kept making it difficult for her to leave.

Truce sat on the kitchen counter watching both of them wash the paint from their hands, occasionally flicking his tail in disdain when water threatened to splash his way. "We'd be better off in the shower," Ryan said.

Greer's head jerked up. Was it only in her head that

he'd just added "together"? "Yes. So I'll just go next door, and—"

"But we'll make do." He tilted her chin before she'd realized he was going to, and took a small damp cloth to a white splotch on her nose and another on her cheek. She lowered her eyes the instant he touched her, and kept them lowered, her soft, dark lashes shadowing her cheeks like tufts of velvet.

Since she obviously had fifty million men in her life, Ryan couldn't figure out why she was skittish with him. Particularly since her cheeks just faintly warmed with color when he touched her: She wasn't indifferent.

"Let's have a glass of wine before we call it a night," he suggested.

Greer dried her hands, debating. Go home, she told herself. Her heart was thundering again, but that was just plain silly. He hadn't made a pass or implied one; they'd shared a neighborly couple of hours and both of them looked like derelicts. Enough of this overreacting to him. So his touch had been infinitely gentle on her cheek. What had she expected him to do? Attack her face with a scouring pad?

She accepted a full wineglass from him, and then he poured his own. Unfortunately, there was no place to sit, between packing crates and a distinct lack of furniture. Ryan solved that by setting a candle in the middle of the hall carpet, and Greer chuckled, flopping down cross-legged next to him.

"To good neighbors." Ryan raised his glass.

She clinked crystal to crystal. "Absolutely." The barren hall had thick carpet and a ceiling light fixture. That was it. After the first two sips Ryan leaned back against the wall and stretched out his legs. Greer leaned against the opposite wall with an equally weary sigh.

"An hour of physical work and I probably won't be able to move tomorrow. I think I'm getting old," she complained ruefully.

Ryan peered at her critically. "I see three freckles but no wrinkles."

"I'm twenty-seven."

"Good Lord. *That* old?"

She couldn't help but stretch out one bare foot to kick him. Only Ryan grabbed her ankle, and before she could pull away he ran his forefinger up and down the sole of her foot. She jerked back with a startled giggle. "Hey," she objected.

"Hey nothing. You're ticklish, all right."

She took a sip of wine, studying him warily over the rim of her glass. "A little," she admitted.

"You said you weren't."

"Fib." Greer hesitated. "I learned to fib a long time ago around men I don't know very well," she said casually. "Actually, that's partly why I came over here tonight."

"To admit you fibbed about being ticklish?" he said gravely.

Greer smiled. "No. Because I..." Her finger slowly traced the rim of the wineglass. Facing the goblins was always the best way. The kiss was still bothering her, and so was her emotional reaction to him. "Friendships are hard to come by. Know that?" she said abruptly.

"Are they?"

"Friendships with members of the opposite sex. Relationships are easy to fall into, friendships less so." Greer paused again. "I value friendships a great deal," she said quietly.

He couldn't help but get the message. Ryan swallowed the last of his wine and set down the glass, his eyes enigmatically dark in the shadowed hall. "You have a man in your life you're serious about?"

"No. I just don't . . . rush into any kind of involvement. Ever."

"Still feeling burned from your ex-husband?"

"It's not that." At *all,* Greer thought fleetingly. She would never again be so naive as to fall for a man who wanted a mother. Over the last year, though, she'd been increasingly aware of the itsy-bitsy paradox she'd made of her life. On the one hand, she'd tried a relationship in which she was the main caretaker, and it had failed miserably. On the other hand, she never allowed men close unless she exerted exactly those same controls. The old resentment over being treated like *prey* and used like a sex object refused to disappear. Yet only occasionally, she felt this restless loneliness . . . a foolish thing. She had plenty of men friends. "How on earth did we get talking about this?" she asked abruptly. "Of all the silly subjects . . ."

Ryan leaned over to refill her glass before she could get up. "One more," he coaxed.

"Well . . ."

She was smiling sleepily by the time he poured the third glass. She was smiling like a woman who badly needed a pillow and a soft mattress . . . and a man to cuddle against. Ryan mentally groaned. The lady was beginning to drive him bananas.

She hadn't told him so, but he had the definite impression she was wary of physical relationships and he couldn't fathom it—unless her ex-husband had been an insensitive jerk in bed. The vibrations didn't feel that way to him, though. When he looked at her, he didn't see a woman who'd been hurt sexually; he saw a woman who hadn't been sexually awakened at all.

He suspected that was sheer male wishful thinking on his part. He couldn't get one thought out of his head: he wished he'd been her first lover. Her only lover. He'd even been jealous of the wall, the way she'd stroked the paint on it. Every damn movement she made was sensual, graceful. The way she pushed back her hair, the way she curled her bare toes; she had small hands that waved expressively when she was talking.

The old sweat shirt and baggy jeans were supposed to conceal the most alluring figure he'd ever laid eyes on. They failed. Her breasts were firm and full, her long legs sleek and feminine, her hips delectably curved, her tummy flat. And no, dammit, it really wasn't just her looks that were driving him nuts. It was Greer. The inside-lady Greer. The sensual woman who was hiding for some unknown reason behind bread-baking sprees.

And from the number of men calling her, she could probably open a successful bakery.

"Ryan."

She was suddenly wearing an exasperated frown. He'd been expecting it, and smiled to himself at the groggy look in her eyes.

"I hate to have to confess this, but I'm not absolutely sure I can get up. Do you know how very rarely I drink three glasses of wine in a row?" Greer asked.

"But then, home's right next door," Ryan observed. "And thanks to the wine, you're going to sleep terrifically tonight." He stood up and offered his hands to her.

She took them and let him pull her up. The wine hadn't made her dizzy, just sleepy. Her eyelids were having a dreadful problem staying open. "We really should finish painting your room," she mentioned idly.

"Tomorrow."

"The cat—"

"I'll get him, Greer."

"This is embarrassing." Her feet just didn't want to get into synchrony, and one hip bumped Ryan's.

"What's embarrassing? You're not trying to impress a bunch of high-class company. We're neighbors."

Greer obediently slumped her head against his shoulder as he steered her toward the door. "That's right." She yawned. "Just neighbors."

She sounded ridiculously happy at the thought. Thoroughly irritated, Ryan paused at her door and had a short internal debate with his conscience. His conscience lost. He didn't really intend to take advantage of her, anyway, but they had to clear up this little difference of opinion on neighbors and . . . neighbors.

"Thank you," she murmured when he pushed open the door for her. "I think I could sleep for a year."

"Greer?"

"Hmmm?" she smiled sleepily up at him.

"I owe you a thank-you for helping."

"No, you don't."

"Yes," he insisted. "And since you offered me a neighborly hug last night as a thank-you, I know you won't mind if I offer you a simple neighborly kiss—" He waited for an imperceptible second. Long enough to appease his grumbling conscience.

Greer's eyes flew wide open, but a second wasn't enough time to gather her scattered wits. Long arms slid under hers, drawing her close to a warm, bare chest with dried paint speckles on it. For some reason, she was staring at those paint speckles when he tilted up her chin.

A warm mouth molded itself over her lips. A light was suddenly too bright somewhere. Greer's eyes closed. Her head tilted helplessly back. His lips wooed hers gently, a tease of lightness and then pressure, a trace of

wine tasted between them that could have been hers . . .
or his.

Her hands rose and then seemed to hover in midair
until his claimed them and gave them a home on his
shoulders. It was a mistake, touching his skin. A who-
cares kind of mistake. He had wonderful skin, warm and
resilient, smooth on his shoulders, muscled on his arms.

She felt as though she'd stepped into a different world.
She'd only stepped into the man, moved closer . . . or he
had. He wasn't like John. He wasn't anything like the
dozens of men she'd kissed in the last few years, who
offered kisses with a tentative smile, prepared for with
cleared throats and organized settings and shy expecta-
tions. She'd freely returned those kinds of kisses, for all
those men.

Not one of them had threatened her. Not one of them
had given her a single reason to believe she couldn't
control the situation if she wanted to.

And not a damn one of them had known what he was
doing, but she hadn't realized that until now. Ryan took
her mouth the way a storm hit on a summer day — languid
sunshine one minute, lightning the next. Restlessly, Greer
stirred, uncertain what to do with a suddenly cloud-fogged
brain. The barometer of her pulse kept dropping, and
then his tongue slipped between her parted teeth. Her
skin heated up wherever he touched.

Hands slid up and down her back, soothing, gentle.
One set of fingers of one hand stole into her hair, cupping
her head. Another slid languorously down her spine to
the curve of her hips. His touch said *mine,* as if he were
identifying every vertebra that belonged to him, slowly,
as if it were a secret. His secret.

He'd set a match to dry tinder. She couldn't in a

thousand years have explained her response. She felt protected in his arms as she'd never in her life felt protected. It wasn't just a sexual sensation, she told herself. And knew darn well it was the sexiest sensation she'd ever felt in her life.

Ryan's lips lingered and then gradually lifted. When she finally raised her eyes she found his staring down at her. Blue. A firelit blue. He wasn't breathing well. "Just a simple thank-you between neighbors," he said gruffly. "The same thing you offered me yesterday. Just . . . a natural expression of affection. Right, Greer?"

"I—"

"You need sleep. I'll bring the cat."

His arms were suddenly gone. She was just standing there, weak in the knees. Thirty seconds later, he dropped a cat in her arms. A purring cat.

That man, she thought dizzily, was . . . tricky.

"I'm going to kill him."

"Hmmm. Your cold sounds much better," Greer said from the depth of the white velvet chair in Marie's office. The chair was in a safe corner, which was important during one of Marie's tirades.

"You think I'm joking?" Marie's office looked as if burglars had just left. Fabrics were strewn over the floor. Papers lay where they had been tossed. And the diminutive blonde was pacing, bunching papers in her hands, and pelting them into the air, her French accent thickening with her fury. "I will leave him and get a divorce and join another firm. *That's* what I will do. He thinks my design is not good enough for his catalog cover?" Marie whirled and shook her finger at Greer. "You thought I would blame *you,* didn't you?"

"Your negligee was beautiful, Marie—but *I* was the one who didn't feel it belonged on the cover. Grant really had nothing to do wi—"

"I *don't* blame you. I blame *him*. And killing is too good for him. Divorce is too good for him. I know exactly what he deserves." Marie collapsed in the chair behind her desk, her golden eyes fiery with rage as she glared at Greer. *"You* look at my husband and you see a small, very proper man, who doesn't even swear so much. *Hah.* He is not so polite between the sheets. You don't think of Grant as a tiger, do you?"

Greer crossed her legs. "Ummm..." Not that the question hadn't been raised before, but it was still difficult to answer tactfully.

"Well, he is. A *tiger*. Even two nights and he can't stand going without. We'll see," Marie said fretfully. "We'll see what a little abstinence does for him. We'll see how long he lasts. He won't *dare* ax one of my designs again. Wait a minute." She bolted out of her chair and skimmed across the debris toward the door. *"You.* Wait here," she called back to Greer.

Alone for at least a minute, Greer yawned. Marie had been ranting for the better part of an hour. For days after her first experience with one of Marie's temper tantrums, Greer had been distraught, disturbed that Marie so freely sputtered private secrets to her, fearing that Marie and Grant were on the verge of a divorce.

Now she was used to it, and absently picked up Marie's new teddy design from the floor where it had been jettisoned. It was simply white ... only Marie had the talent to make simply white look wicked. And next to it lay a basic pair of pajamas ... in a luscious coral silk, with coral satin piping on hem and cuffs and a mandarin collar. Basic, yes. But utterly luxurious next to the skin.

When Marie didn't instantly return, Greer automatically started to straighten up the office—at least until a woosh of satin was plopped over her head. Gingerly, she pushed back enough of the fabric to see out.

Marie was smiling. "For you," she said magnanimously. "You think I want that anywhere around here? Take it home and keep it out of my sight. It will fit you to absolute perfection. You know I can look at any woman and know her size. Your figure was made for it."

"Mmm," Greer murmured and divested herself of the pink satin and cream lace. For a moment, she stared at the negligee that had caused so much trouble, thinking vaguely that the lovely thing had been created to cause trouble. Of one kind or another. "Marie, you know I'm not the type to wear this sort of thing."

Marie muttered something in French, which Grant had one time translated loosely as "horsefeathers."

"Regardless, I don't want you to give this to me, Marie. The design is wonderful, and if we could use a less expensive fabric—"

"I will *never* use the design again. *Never*. Oh, that *man.*" Marie, huffing, flopped back in her chair, five feet two of steam and energy.

"Grant loved the design," Greer mentioned.

"He does not appreciate me. He has never appreciated me. I sent all the way to Bordeaux for that lace..."

"Which you knew ahead of time would make the negligee impossibly expensive."

"And I told Barney I wanted *satin*. Not *this*—" She picked up the white camisole that Greer had placed on the desk and pushed it to the floor again. "Not *like* satin. Not *wash-and-wear*. I am so tired of wash-and-wear fabrics I could scream. I *hate* fake. Real satin must be treated like a baby; it requires a lot of trouble, a lot of time, but then! *Then,* when you see what it does next to a woman's skin..."

"But that also brought up the price," Greer reminded her gently.

Marie wasn't paying attention. "I wanted to create something it would take courage to wear. A little daring. Real élan."

"Would you wear it yourself?" Greer questioned.

Marie glanced at Greer in surprise. "Of course I would not wear it myself. I would look flat like a wall if I put that on. It would trail on the floor after me as if I were a little girl playing dress-up. You think I am stupid? You think I've kept Grant in my life by being stupid? He knows what he's got when the lights are out, but when they're still on, my darling, he can't be sure. A little subtle padding, a few carefully sewn tucks, a flounce here and a bow there to distract him from what I don't have."

"That's exactly why your designs are so brilliant, Marie," Greer said soothingly, tactfully not mentioning that one didn't divorce a man for whom one was willing to resort to such deviousness. "You have a gift for hiding a woman's worst points and accenting her best. Exactly why we've been so successful. Grant was just telling Barney that yesterday."

"Grant," Marie scoffed. "My husband knows nothing. *Nothing.*" She hesitated. "He said that, though?"

"He said that."

"I am *not* forgiving him for that negligee not being on the cover."

"Of course you aren't." Greer unconsciously fingered the pink satin negligee before carefully placing it on the chair and moving toward the door. "He was upstairs with the girls yesterday. There was something wrong with one of the sewing machines; Rachel said it was usable, but Grant told her to forget it—that you'd find one stitch out of place. He told her you were a perfectionist . . . and that if she didn't feel the same way, the door was available to her."

"I *am* a perfectionist," Marie said proudly.

"Of course you are."

"That Rachel . . . she can be careless if I'm not looking right over her shoulder every minute."

"I think that's why Grant made a special trip up here while you were out with that cold."

"Hmmm." Marie's eyes narrowed as Greer took another step backward. "Take the negligee, take it, take it. Stop fussing. You know I meant for you to have it."

"Marie—"

"Take that thing. Immediately." Marie waved at the negligee, and then briskly stood, picked up the garment, and pushed it into Greer's arms again. As an afterthought, she reached up to press a kiss on both Greer's cheeks in the French way. "You are a good friend. I want you to have it, and wear it for a very special man, yes? It suits you exactly. I knew the minute I thought of the design." She added, "And when I divorce Grant, I will start my own business and you will come with me. We will make our own firm. All women. No men. Not *one*."

Later, Greer was working in her office on ad copy, the negligee folded carefully and out of sight, when Grant paused in her doorway, nervously tightening his tie.

"Safe," she said shortly.

"You're sure?"

"Positive."

Twenty minutes after that, Marie and Grant passed her office on the way out. Greer suppressed a grin. It was only three in the afternoon, yet she knew the two were leaving for the day, and not for business. Their arguments inevitably ended the same way, and Greer had no doubts that they would both come in yawning the next day.

She returned to her work and barely lifted her head again until five. The ad copy was done, and sales figures took the rest of the afternoon. She'd started a study months before on colors related to sales in lingerie. Women assumed men considered black and red sexy, and yet the men who bought lingerie for their wives invariably picked out white. Pastels appeared to confuse men so that they had difficulty choosing, but women always had a favorite soft color they adopted for their own. Putting that all together and making recommendations to Grant was part of Greer's job.

By the time she'd cleared her desk and grabbed her raincoat and purse, she'd almost convinced herself she'd forgotten the negligee. She hesitated and then pushed open the cardboard box, fingering the delicate satin and lace wistfully.

How many studies had she done on lingerie in the last five years? And all of them had led to the same conclusion: Women bought beautiful lingerie to make a statement for them: Hold me, warm me, I *need* to be touched. A woman had a secret wish to be pampered, a wish that she couldn't say out loud and that she didn't *want* to say out loud.

The negligee would have been all wrong for the cover of Love Lace, but not for reasons Greer could have explained to the men. The pink satin whispered, *I am a strong sexual woman, and I don't mind singing it from the rooftops*. Wearing this negligee would require confidence. Confidence in one's own sexuality, confidence and enough courage to flaunt one's sexuality, to entice, to boldly seduce. Few women had that kind of confidence.

Or is it you, Greer? she thought absently. Maybe you were expressing your own insecurities when you rejected that design for the catalog cover. Maybe other women feel perfectly free to play the aggressor in a sexual relationship. This is hardly the nineteenth century . . . maybe the problem lies in *you*.

She closed the box, slid it under her arm, and picked up her purse again. She would tuck the negligee away in a drawer at home. She took it anyway.

Ryan's embrace had preyed on her mind all day. His *neighborly* embrace. The man disturbed her. Cream lace on pink satin disturbed her.

Going home to clean out the cat's litter box was the best method she knew of clearing the mind of disturbing fancies.

Following that, she had a date with Daniel. Come to think of it, Ryan had been listening when she'd made that date, the first night she'd met her neighbor.

Greer banished Ryan from her mind. Thinking about Daniel was safer. Daniel was a sweetie. And Daniel wouldn't arouse pink-satin daydreams in anyone's mind.

# Chapter Five

THE BRA FELT just a smidgen tight around her left breast.
Greer sucked in her ribs on an inhale, and twisted on the
exhale. It helped. Peering at her reflection in her dresser
mirror, she was relieved to see that the lopsided fit of
the bra didn't show. Her dress was a sheath of royal blue
with a mandarin collar and gold embroidery from neckline to hem in back. The Chinese style made her figure
look almost petite. Beneath the dress, she was wearing
a violet half-slip and a new bra that was one of Marie's
best-selling designs—except for this particular castoff.
The seamstress had made one cup slightly smaller than
the other.

If she'd guessed ahead of time how strangely it would
fit, she would have changed bras. Unfortunately, she

could already hear Daniel's knock. She picked up her glasses. As expected, when she opened the door, Daniel was wearing his. Though she rarely wore her glasses except for driving, she knew Daniel felt more comfortable when she had them on.

"I'm sorry I'm late, Greer. Really sorry. My boss did it to me again—just at five, he came in with a mound of work..."

Daniel was blond, tall, and lanky, and he had trouble deciding what to do with his long arms when he was nervous. Greer gave him a quick hello kiss, then rushed into the kitchen to fill Truce's dish before leaving. "I've told you before, you know," she called back gently. "Nothing's going to happen if you simply tell him you'll do the work first thing in the morning, Daniel. He's not going to fire you; you're too good at what you do. You've got the right to say no when he makes unreasonable demands."

By the time she returned to the living room, Daniel was running a hand through his hair. "I try."

"I know you do." She smiled reassuringly at him.

"You're not irritated that I'm late?"

"Of course I'm not irritated."

Tucking her key in her purse, she opened the apartment door, still chattering to Daniel... until she saw the slim, svelte blonde coming out of Ryan's apartment.

The woman was pretty. Not beautiful, not voluptuous, not overly made up, just... pretty. And she was one of those small-breasted women who could wear anything. In this case a loose silky dress draped from shoulder to hip and caught casually at the waist with a double belt. The style would have made Greer look like a hooker. On the blonde, it was casual, attractive, and stylish.

She was laughing.

So was Ryan, just behind her. His chest wasn't naked today, but clothed in crisp white linen and a tie, which he fussed with until he noticed Greer.

". . . anyway, Ry, I appreciate your getting me out of a bind this evening," the blonde was saying.

"I thought—that is, if you wanted to, Greer, we could go to Lombardi's," Daniel suggested.

*Why* was Ryan tying that tie as if he were just getting dressed? Jealousy pierced Greer as if she'd just walked barefoot over a bed of nails.

Ryan took one long look at Daniel and felt every muscle stiffen. *Endearing*. The dude had that *endearing* look women loved, and he had a tiny glaze of lip gloss on his cheek. Fresh. Greer looked edible in royal blue to the neck, the soft fabric draped subtly over her figure in a way that hinted at luscious mysteries. Her hair was sleeked back, giving her an air of sophistication, showing off her profile. He hadn't seen her wearing glasses before and immediately took a dislike to them. The oversized frames did not detract from her looks, but they hid the expression in her eyes. All he could see were huge brown mirrors, reflecting back, giving nothing away.

"Lombardi's?" Ryan said smoothly. "We're going there, too."

Daniel's head whipped around to stare at Ryan in surprise, and he found himself facing Ryan's outstretched hand. "Ryan McCullough here. Greer's neighbor. I just heard you mention Lombardi's. We'll probably see you at the restaurant."

Ryan's blonde looked momentarily disconcerted, and then chuckled, a low, musical sound. "Ry, I thought you said—not that it matters."

After shaking Daniel's hand, Ryan stepped back with a hand at his date's back. "This is Leigh Neuman. Laughlin's personnel manager. She has the unenviable job of wining and dining new employees. Like me, poor woman."

"Nice to meet you, Leigh," Daniel said politely.

"Leigh—Greer—" In the middle of that introduction, Ryan snapped his fingers. "If we're all going to the same restaurant, we may as well share the drive. It's a little distance, isn't it?" He added quickly, "Not, of course, that I would want to interrupt a private dinner."

Daniel had a stricken look that Greer knew signified a bad attack of insecurity around strangers. "Well..." he started nervously.

"I understand it's nearly a half-hour drive. I haven't been there before, and I was a little worried about getting lost. My car's right outside, if you're familiar with the directions, Dan? We can always separate when we get there, if you like."

They didn't separate at the restaurant. By the time the four of them had piled into a booth, they were all chattering away like long-lost friends. Daniel was talking to Ryan as if he'd never had a man friend he could share interests with before, and Leigh was bubbling on to Greer about her fiancé and about how Ryan had been kind enough to switch their arranged business dinner on the spur of the moment so she wouldn't miss a date with her fiancé on the following Thursday.

"It's foolish, the company policy of taking new people out to dinner. With Ryan, of course I don't mind, but I've gotten into some fair pickles in the past, trying to make conversation with a few stuffed shirts who couldn't figure out what they were doing in the company of a strange woman. It's supposed to be a welcome to the company, but right now it just doesn't make sense. The new building's not completed; we've got tons of new people running around; and Norm doesn't appreciate my spending half my evenings with strange men..."

"I can understand that," Greer said. Leigh was all bubbles and laughter, impossible not to like.

Why Lombardi's served Chinese food, no one could figure out. The atmosphere was strictly Italian, with a foaming fountain in the center of the restaurant, candles on the tables, and a trio of musicians in one corner trying to coax people to the dance floor with everything from polkas to rock.

The four of them drank rice wine and ate egg rolls until the entrées were served, and then dishes and arms rapidly crossed as they sampled each other's dinners. It was only when Greer was perfectly stuffed and had slipped off her shoes under the table that she realized she was sitting next to Ryan. She was also sitting next to Daniel, of course, but they were in a semicircular booth, and she really didn't remember Ryan climbing in next to her. Nor did she know exactly why his thigh happened to be touching hers.

Particularly when Daniel was a polite six inches away, his face flushed with wine. It took a great deal for Daniel to shed his inhibitions and join a gathering of strangers, and Ryan had made that happen.

Ryan. Her friendly neighbor. The only one at the table who had miraculously avoided conversation with her for the last two hours. He'd talked to Daniel and he'd talked to Leigh, just not directly to Greer. After the waitress served an after-dinner saki, Ryan turned to his date.

"That trio's going to get depressed if someone doesn't take up a little space on their dance floor," he told her.

Leigh laughed. "No problem."

The dance number was slow. Daniel looked uncertainly at Greer, and she almost sighed. Most of the time

Daniel's shy ways were appealing. "Let's," she agreed, and they followed the others to the dance floor.

Actually, Daniel was an excellent dancer. Like other introverted people, he came into his own when not threatened with a verbal situation. He'd learned to dance properly, one hand at her waist, the other holding hers loosely—which didn't distract in any way from his rhythmic skill. "He's nice, your neighbor," Daniel said quietly.

"Yes."

"I rarely feel that comfortable with people on a first meeting, but then most people don't seem that interested in accounting systems."

"Yes," she echoed.

"I'm glad we came with them." Daniel's face took on an immediate soft flush, as if aware he might have said something tactless. "Not that I wouldn't have preferred an evening alone with you—"

Greer was running out of patience. Daniel's palm was getting damp, annoying her. The left cup of her bra was also annoying her. Having a totally pleasant dinner was, for some unknown reason, also annoying her. She had removed her glasses at the table—she didn't need them for the dance floor. But she couldn't see over Daniel's shoulder to Ryan and Leigh.

The number ended and an old-fashioned fox trot began. Daniel smiled, automatically changing rhythms, when Ryan touched his shoulder.

"You don't mind if we switch for a dance, do you?" Ryan asked. "I can see you know what you're doing on the floor, and I thought I'd give Leigh a break."

Which really wasn't very flattering, Greer thought vaguely, but Daniel was already steering Leigh around the floor. She caught a quick glimpse of Ryan's face before his arms came around her, but the dance floor was dark, and she could have misread that innocent expression.

A minute and a half into the dance, and she knew the devil should be so innocent. She also figured out rapidly that Ryan had never learned to dance the fox trot and that his feet were size twenty. Actually, she was fairly amazed at his clumsiness.

Not that he didn't compensate for his lack of expertise, and promptly. Very slowly, he slid his arms around her waist, which would have left her own waving in midair unless she put them around his neck. Just as slowly, he pulled her close and started shuffling. The combo was playing another fox trot. Ryan was playing love songs. Lazily erotic love songs.

His muscled thigh nudged between her legs and simply moved back and forth in a rhythm that was slow, erotic, and intimate. Deliberately intimate. Greer was strongly inclined to take him over her knee and certainly wished his mother had done so when he was younger, but for at least a few moments she couldn't do much of anything. Rippling, sultry waves of desire were clogging her brain. The mold of hip to hip was bad enough, but he kept . . . rubbing. In rhythm. A primal mating rhythm. And his hands started making slow-moving circles somewhere low on her spine. Very low on her spine.

Daniel and Leigh seemed to be on the other side of the dance floor.

Greer's throat was suddenly dry. "Ryan." She tried to lift her head. His palm gently pushed her cheek back to his chest. Her eyes were on a level with the shadowed length of his throat. She could see the beat of blood in the veins just below that smooth flesh.

"Sssh, Greer." Then he whispered with counterfeit

nervousness, "For heaven's sakes, don't move. I don't know how to do this kind of dance, and I don't want to step on your feet."

"Ryan."

"Hmmm?"

She whispered close to his ear, "I can be made a fool of once. Maybe even twice. But if you're trying to pass this off as more neighborly affection, I just wanted to warn you up front that you're very close to a kick in the shins."

His eyes glittered down at her, full-of-nonsense blue. Dangerous blue. "Now, Greer. Don't tell me simple affection isn't possible between two people of opposite sex. Isn't that what you were trying to tell me the night we met?"

"This is *not* the same thing."

"Maybe not for you, but *I'm* feeling extremely affectionate right now. And since the song just ended, I'd appreciate it if you'd stick around for another. Walking back to the table in this particular physical condition wouldn't bother me, but I'm afraid it might be obvious to your Daniel." He shook his head gravely. "He might get the wrong impression. That I want you like hell, for instance."

Greer flushed, tried to pull away but failed to escape from arms that suddenly held her with gentle but unmistakable firmness. "What are you trying to do to me?" she asked helplessly.

"Wake you up, love." He said it so low he was almost certain she hadn't heard it. She was fighting hard to keep her body a distance from his. So hard.

Ryan had felt a moment's guilt where her Daniel was concerned, but not too much. He'd watched the two interact over dinner long enough to be certain he wasn't

poaching on another man's territory, and long enough to
evaluate Daniel as an intelligent man, not bad looking
and not unkind. But physically, he clearly stirred Greer
about as much as used dish water. Ryan wasn't stealing
anything that belonged to anyone else.

Greer's heart, pressed against his shirt, seemed to be
doing somersaults. Her nipples were hard and hot, and
he could feel them through two layers of fabric—her
clothes and his. She jumped every time his thigh touched
just so between hers . . . and then she couldn't jump, because he held her too close to give her the chance.

If she'd seriously argued, he would have released her.
Maybe. He wanted to believe that a speck of honor was
alive and well in him somewhere, but her closeness was
having disastrous effects on his principles.

And when she suddenly and totally relaxed, he doubted
very much that he could ever let her go. Her body went
supple and pliant in his arms; her cheek rested in the
furrow at the base of his throat; her fingers slowly climbed
above his shirt collar and into his hair . . . and then stiffened, as if she'd suddenly became aware of what she
was doing.

"The dance is almost over," he whispered casually.
Tentatively, she relaxed again, as if reassured. He had
the fleeting sensation of taming a wild creature. So unwilling, so wary, yet her body had turned warm, melt-
ingly warm. One finger again traveled up into his hair.
Just one. Very slowly, he caressed the curves of her back,
down again to her hips, and he heard her let her breath
out in a rush. Gently, he pressed a butterfly kiss on her
temple.

She liked that. She murmured something. Not a word,
more a helpless purr of pleasure. His hand roamed slowly
up her side . . . and then—the devil made him do it—

his thumb strayed to the underside of her breast. Her head jerked up instantly, her face flushed and her eyes sleepy with arousal, dark, almost wild.

"We *have* to sit down," she said frantically.

He kept his voice calm, soothing. "Your Daniel's nice."

"Ryan, I—"

"And he's certainly not your heavy breather. He couldn't possibly have been making those phone calls."

She looked startled. "I knew that."

"I didn't." The dance was almost over; he knew she was determined to withdraw from him this time. "What the hell are you wearing?" he asked to divert her.

She stiffened. "Pardon?"

"Are you wired for sound?" He pressed her cheek back to his shoulder and continued to shuffle. "That kind of bra has to be uncomfortable. Why the hell do you wear it?"

"I beg your—"

"Now, Greer. We're just neighbors. Friends. No need to be embarrassed around me. In fact, you were the first one to bring up the subject of underwear, weren't you?"

The dance wasn't over, but Greer had had enough. She pulled away from him and made her way back to the table, her cheeks so hot they felt on fire.

Daniel returned to the table equally flushed. Fifteen minutes later, they were driving home. The men talked the entire time, dialogue tossed from front seat to back, with Leigh occasionally joining in. Greer was far too unsettled to listen. Her body was sending out pre-flu messages, alternately hot and cold, oddly trembling. Only it wasn't the flu season. And what*ever* had possessed her to respond to Ryan like that on the dance floor? She wasn't certain whether she was embarrassed or ashamed of herself.

She was absolutely certain that she was furious with her neighbor.

Leigh had left her car near Ryan's parking spot. As Daniel strolled with Greer up the walk, she could hear the other woman's car door being closed, the engine starting over low, throaty laughter between Leigh and Ryan. Before Daniel had even pushed open the outside door, Ryan's heels were clicking on the pavement behind them.

"I'll dig out that study I told you about, if you think it would be any help," Ryan told Daniel as he fished his apartment key out of his pocket.

"I don't want to put you to any trouble..."

"No trouble. And no hurry either," Ryan assured him, and winked.

He promptly disappeared, quietly closing his door to leave Daniel and Greer in privacy. Greer, for no reason at all, felt doubly furious. Actually, she knew the reason. It was that wink. That condescending wink. As if *inviting* Daniel to try out a passionate clinch with Greer.

She couldn't think of anything else the whole time Daniel worked up to his good-night kiss. While he methodically slipped off his glasses and started clearing his throat, Greer debated whether or not to ask him in. They'd been out several times in the last few months. One of these nights she'd planned to... well, at least *see*. Daniel's kisses were warm, undemanding, lovely. He obviously wanted more. She really wouldn't know how she felt about him until she tested it out. To hell with her neighbor. Daniel's shyness was thawing; he might just be a very good man if she could coax him out of his shell.

Ryan had evidently already coaxed him halfway out of his shell. Greer was still mulling the problem over when Daniel startled her with his kiss. There was a tiny trace of aggression in the way he swung his arms around Greer . . . though she could taste the breath mint he'd popped into his mouth as they left the restaurant.

Her head tilted back, and she closed her eyes and felt Daniel's moist lips touch hers. The taste was interesting, kind of like a peppermint-soaked sponge. She'd have given up her life savings to feel some kind of wild response to his kiss, but it was like that small problem of silk purses and sows' ears. Dammit. Daniel's touch was . . . clumsy. His tongue flickered out like a tiny serpent and, thank God, almost instantly withdrew. "You're so beautiful, Greer," he whispered. "Don't worry; I'm not about to press you. I know you're not the kind of woman who wants to rush things."

A moment later, he left. Behind the locked door of her apartment, Greer tossed down her purse, tugged off her shoes, and flopped into the couch. Truce instantly soared to her lap and settled in with approving purrs for her return. She patted the cat absently, then stood up, letting Truce drape himself around her neck, and paced.

Through thin walls, she heard a door opening, Ryan's voice. Then Daniel's.

She paced some more. That *man*. He wasn't just tricky; he was becoming seriously dangerous. Whatever happened to rules? When a man was coming on to you, he was supposed to play by a certain set of rules. On a chessboard, there were few aggressive moves Greer couldn't counter. In life, the same.

Ryan wasn't playing fair.

Monday night, she didn't arrive home from work until ten after seven. Love Lace had abruptly decided to gear up for the coming trade show. Greer had figured out a long time ago that people in the garment industry thrived on seasonal frenzies rather than advance preparations— actually, so did she.

Except that the air conditioning had been off all day; she was hot, irritable, and tired after nine hours at her desk. Dropping her purse on the counter, she headed directly for the shower, peeling off clothes en route.

Underneath a deluge of soothing tepid water, she felt at least four of two dozen tense muscles begin to relax. Dinner and a few hours with her feet up would do the rest. She was rinsing her hair when the telephone rang.

Afraid it was her crank caller, she tensed instantly . . . and calmed down just as instantly, knowing it was her mother. She always called her mother at seven o'clock on Mondays, and when the ritual varied by even a few minutes, Greer's mother worried. Hurriedly flicking off the faucet as the phone rang again, Greer stepped out of the shower, groping blindly for a towel.

Her eyes blinked open. She had shoved the towels in the washer at six o'clock that morning; she hadn't thought to replace them. The phone rang again. Shivering, she raced out to the living room stark naked, Truce standing guard by the phone with his tail switching, limpid eyes interestedly following Greer's drips all over the carpet.

"Hello. Mom?" Some days her breather called three times, sometimes none. Although she was sure it was her mother, she didn't feel the surge of apprehension disappear until she heard the familiar voice. Greer relaxed, pushing back her damp hair with a grin, shivering. "No, I'm fine. I'm sorry I didn't call on time; I hadn't forgotten. I was going to call within another—"

The apartment door flew open. Greer's jaw dropped in shock.

Ryan barreled in on a clear beeline for her telephone.

He was wearing suit pants and an unbuttoned shirt that waved around his thighs; his feet were bare. Nothing on him, though, was quite as bare as she was, and the look in his eyes was nothing's-going-to-stop-me determined.

Their eyes met, clashed, collided. He couldn't possibly not have noticed her dripping bare skin, but his hand was still firmly extended, demanding the receiver. Greer's mother was chatting about gardening.

Greer dropped promptly behind the couch, the phone to her ear, furiously waving him away. Her fingers were weaving on the right side of the couch; his face appeared over the top on the left side.

"You're not talking to anyone. Is it him?" he demanded.

Amazing. Her breasts could blush. So could her navel. Would you get *out* of here, she mouthed frantically, and finally managed to interject a comment into her mother's monologue. "That's wonderful, Mom. Really. I . . ."

Ryan disappeared. Within seconds, the door to her apartment closed again. Cautiously, she peeked over the back of the couch. "Of *course* I've been listening," she told her mother indignantly. "You were telling me about Mrs. Inger's arthritis—"

He was gone.

Later, when she was fully dressed and fed, and the dishes washed and the cat petted, and the clock had long ago ticked past her bedtime hour, Greer was still sitting on the couch, thinking.

Around one, she finally figured out that the sole reason Ryan had come over was to protect her from her breather. She went to bed, yawning with overtired exasperation. She hadn't expected him to come over for any other reason, of course.

Except that he'd come on like a freight train when

they were dancing. He'd packed kisses like explosives, and in more subtle ways showed a very definite interest. For three days after that, they hadn't seen each other, and when they did she was naked.

But then, he hadn't even blinked twice when he saw her naked.

Half her life, Greer would have given gold for men who didn't look at her figure.

She plumped up the pillow for the fourth time, pushed Truce off the bed for the third time, and stared at a night-black ceiling with her eyes wide open. *Don't you fall in love with him, lady. Stick to the kind of men you can handle.*

Her conscience was always good for a pep talk. Greer was too honest to kid herself. Ryan . . . she couldn't handle him. And her feelings around him . . . she wasn't very good at handling those, either. Moorings shifted; landmarks disappeared; mental fogs rolled in when he was around.

Greer was safe just as she was. In time, perhaps, she'd want marriage again, but to a man she felt comfortable with. Ryan didn't make her feel comfortable; she felt perfectly miserable around him. Those blue eyes of his invited wanton, deliciously decadent behavior, but Greer wasn't playmate material. She'd never *played,* not where her sexual feelings were concerned. Sex was a serious business. And if she hadn't taken it seriously, she would have been used more than once in her life.

Only Ryan made her feel as if it were . . . fun. As if touch had to do with laughter. As if kisses had to do with mischief. As if fooling an entire crowded restaurant had been . . . exciting. As if she were a different kind of woman, a woman who enjoyed enticing, and low-voiced laughter, and private, intimate teasing . . .

 *Goose. If you ever tried to play that role, they'd laugh you off the stage, Greer. Go to sleep.*

 She did.

# Chapter Six

"STOP," GREER WHISPERED into the telephone. "Would you just *stop*? Leave me *alone!*"

She put down the phone and promptly burst into tears. Her breather had called *incessantly* this week. Dragging a hand through her hair, she paced the living room in her stockinged feet, her eyes blinded by tears. She was still dressed for work, in a tan and white skirt and tan blouse. She had kicked off her shoes and tossed her white jacket on the couch hours before. She'd worked like a slave ever since she'd come home.

She didn't normally work on Friday nights, much less schedule a follow-up meeting with Ray for a Saturday morning. Only because it *was* Ray had she agreed. The man had been so damned impossible to work with this last week. She'd snatched at the chance to establish some kind of decent professional relationship with him.

After fifteen straight hours of work, her nerves were on the tensile edge of exhaustion. Her breather calling at this late hour had been the last straw after an impossibly long day. The tears kept dripping, and fear filled the weary corners of her mind. Most Friday nights she went out. *How* could he have known she was home on this one?

Unless he was watching. Heart pounding, Greer whirled around to face the living-room windows, but the draperies were closed. Or nearly. There was a thin strip of darkness where they didn't quite meet, and she rushed over to pull those ends together.

Fresh moisture brimmed in her eyes. Grabbing Truce and a bag of knitting, she let herself out of the apartment, leaned against the bare white wall in the hall, and took one calming breath after another. *Why do you persist in believing you're safer out here?*

Because safety wasn't the issue. This was a matter of putting distance between herself and that white wall phone, that *man*. And the caller was a man. She knew the sound of a man's deep breathing.

With a loud, emphatic sigh, she sat on the hall carpet with her legs tucked under her and grabbed her knitting needles and a long strand of pale green yarn from her tapestry bag. Click, click. She sniffed. More click-clicks, until an entire row of Robin's sweater was finished, that row a little tear-blotched but basically straight.

When the hall door opened at the bottom of the steps, she jumped three feet, still sniffing.

"Greer?"

Before she could blink, Ryan's work boots had bounded up the steps and settled in front of her. She did *not* want to see him. The man had run her through an emotional maze all week, darting in and out of her life as if he belonged there. Depending on him was asking for trouble. And that was half the darn problem anyway. He was incredibly easy to depend on.

"Hey."

He was also difficult to ignore. "Hi," she said brightly.

His long legs bent at the knees, jeans straining to accommodate the muscles in his thighs. Apart from jeans and work boots and a blue work shirt, he was wearing impatience like an outer garment. She couldn't see his face, since she was busy click-clicking with her knitting needles, but she could smell his mood, the way a fawn could sniff a hunter's closeness. "You wear jeans more often than any engineer I ever heard of," she remarked casually, and refrained from sniffing one last time. Furiously, she blinked away the last hint of tears. "And don't you ever keep regular hours? You realize it's nearly midnight?"

He didn't move toward her. He didn't touch her, but he didn't move so much as an inch away, either. "You're all right?"

"You told me one time that mechanical engineers are high-class grease monkeys. How did you put it? 'A mechanical engineer plays with a drawing board half the time. The other half he has to figure out why,' I quote, 'his half-assed designs didn't work.'" Knit-purl, knit-purl. "Is that why you're so late?"

"Because of a half-assed design? In a way." He paused, and then his voice continued, as soothing as butter, calming, reassuring. For a moment. "They can teach you a great deal in school about mathematical precision. Nothing about the human factor of blending man and machine. Efficiency, safety, timing—those problems can't be solved on the most brilliant man's drawing board. Exactly why I opted for the mechanical end of engineering. And you're excellent at doing that," he added abruptly.

"Doing what?"

"Getting a man to talk about his favorite subjects. But you can stow it with me, Greer; I'm no Daniel. Now what the hell are you doing out here? As if I didn't know."

"It was hot in the apartment. Something's wrong with that air conditioner again."

"You've been crying."

"You'd cry, too, if you'd just dropped four stitches."

"How many times has he called today?"

"No one has called," Greer assured him, salvaging another straggly length of yarn that Truce was trying to paw.

"Would you stop that?" he said irritably. "Look at me."

"Nope."

He almost smiled at the stubborn tilt to her chin. He'd seen her when she left for work that morning, all crisp efficiency in her white blazer and white pumps, her hips swinging briskly in the tan and white A-line skirt on the way to her car. Her outfit hadn't changed so drastically since then, only her expression. Now, she looked crisp, efficient, and stubborn.

He'd seen that look a lot this week. In terms of attire, he'd seen her in her bag-lady gear, dressed alluringly for a date, in the pastel business suits that showed off her legs, and that once he wasn't likely to forget, naked. Greer was a lot of women in one, but the image that was undoubtedly going to drive him over the edge was the slightly irrational woman with the big brown eyes and the stubborn streak.

If he'd been a less obstinate man, he might have given

up over the last seven days. As if he could have stopped himself from falling in love with her. Her quick humor, her compassion, her keen mind, her love-every-day spirit . . . she gave so much to him, without half trying.

That Greer was his, he already knew. Convincing her of that was proving a battle of wits, only Ryan was just beginning to realize that the harder she fought, the more success he was having. It had been tough understanding that. His engineer's rational brain rejected the off-the-wall premise as illogical, but then he'd had to try to think a little like Greer.

Silently rising to his feet with a frown, he disappeared inside his apartment and returned moments later with a small box. He hunched over and started setting up a marble chessboard.

Greer flicked the yarn over her needle, only mildly shaking her head when she saw what he was doing. "First of all, that's not necessary. It's past midnight and you must be tired. Second, contrary to outward appearances, I do not require a baby-sitter. And last, you really don't want to play chess."

"Why not?" Ryan had won tournament after tournament in college. He might be a little rusty, but he was good enough so she'd never know when he let her beat him.

In the first game, Greer beat him in fifteen minutes. In the second game it took her nearly twenty minutes. And when Ryan set up the board a third time, he had that distinctly sour look that men get when they've been bested in any competitive sport—by a woman.

"You don't play *rationally*," he told her.

"I'll try to improve—that is, if you're not giving up?"

"Your move," he said flatly. His eyes met hers, and her lashes quickly lowered. She understood that he wasn't giving up. Not in chess, and not in the fancy little game of neighbor-friend they'd been playing for almost two weeks.

Ryan waited, carefully. In the process of concentrating on the game, her tears had dried, and the pinched look had left her features. She was getting a disgustingly innocent little spark of triumph in her eyes. He'd sat cross-legged for the game. Greer, after fidgeting with her skirt, had gradually given in to comfort and was lying on her stomach, her legs swinging in the air behind her, her chin cupped in her hands between moves.

A half-hour into the third game, he saw the rare opportunity to steal her rook and did.

Greer glanced up. "How could I have been so stupid?" she asked mournfully.

"You aren't. You're trying—most insultingly—to throw the game. Probably out of pity."

"I was *not*. I've never thrown a game in my life."

"Fine." He whisked one of her bishops off the board with his next move. "Did you call the police?"

She tensed up like a taut rubber band. "Ryan, there is *nothing* else I can do. There is nothing else *anyone* can do. I've had my phone number changed twice now, and I refuse to have the line tapped for the rest of my life. Now I have no choice except to ignore him."

"You have to find out who's doing it."

"I've tried figuring that out, dammit." She slipped his queen off the board with her knight and then looked up guiltily. "Sorry."

"That queen was wide open. Don't apologize." Ryan wasn't even looking at the board. "*Someone* is making those calls, Greer. Some man. Maybe a neighbor, maybe one of the men upstairs, maybe someone you work with. You must have *some* idea—"

"Well, I don't. And we've been through this."

"On the surface. We never got down to the nitty-gritty." He leaned over the board and touched her chin to make her look up at him. "Cards on the table now, and don't fuss. Maybe a man you refused to sleep with? A man you turned down who's trying to get back at you?"

She pushed his hand away from her chin and pulled herself up to her knees, concentrating fiercely on the chessboard. "For heaven's sake," she said in a low voice, "if every man that I'd refused to sleep with called me up to harass me . . . I've dated my share of men, for heaven's sake. Was I supposed to say yes every time I was asked?"

Very quietly Ryan said, "I don't think you've said yes to any man since you divorced your husband."

Greer sucked in a little air. Her lungs seemed to need it. "How many men I've slept with has nothing to do with—"

"It could have a great deal to do with it, Greer."

"It doesn't have to be a man anyway," she said crossly.

"You believe it is, or you wouldn't be scared out of your wits every time the phone rings." When she didn't answer, Ryan let out a mental sigh. He watched her fingers tremble as they moved a pawn, and said very gently, very firmly, "You're staying at my place tonight."

She dropped the pawn. "Don't be silly."

"All right. Then I'll stay with you at your place."

"That *wasn't* what I meant." Greer gave up trying to follow the game. "You caught me in a little crying jag, I admit that. That hardly means I'm falling apart. In fact, that cry was delightful."

"Delightful?" The word clearly took him by surprise.

"It happens. Not often, but every once in a while. An occasional good cry can let out an awful lot of excess emotional baggage. This day was the pits. My breather's been driving me nuts. Now, I don't know what men do when they've just plain had enough—throw temper tantrums? Hurl things against the wall? Surely everyone's entitled to a simple rotten mood?"

"We walk," he snapped.

"Pardon?"

Ryan uncrossed his legs and surged to his feet, and then reached down to pull Greer to hers. "When a man's just plain had enough, he walks. Or this one does. Where are your shoes?"

She opened her lips to remind him politely that it was now past one in the morning, then hesitated, felt a familiar sensation of being tied up in knots, and abruptly ducked into her apartment to fetch her shoes and put the cat inside. All right. They'd walk.

In some areas, she was discovering, Ryan could be just a tiny bit bullheaded. He made her laugh; he made her think; he made her feel any number of uncomfortable emotions; but when he got that certain look in his eyes, arguments bounced off him like marshmallows off a brick wall.

She'd been running into that side of him all week. On Wednesday, for instance, her niece, Robin, had come over. Andrew had naturally trailed after his runaway daughter, and they were exchanging their usual clipped dialogue when Ryan had appeared at the door with a measuring cup in his hand. She'd stared at him in total surprise. "I need a cup of salt," he'd told her, all boyish neighbor. After shoving the cup into her hand, he'd settled in next to Andrew, and hadn't left until he'd clearly established that her brother-in-law wasn't the kind to make crank calls.

There'd been two other times that week when the

phone had rung, and Ryan had appeared from nowhere. One of those calls had been The Breather, and Ryan had parked in her living room the rest of the evening, an immovable rock, that same stubborn angle to his chin.

Actually, that evening they'd had a wonderful time, talking until a ridiculously late hour. If he would just *stop* thinking she needed a keeper, all because of her foolish phone calls. She didn't need a keeper; she'd never needed a keeper.

And worse, she was getting used to him being around when she was scared out of her wits. The *last* thing she wanted was to become attached to the man, and she was terribly afraid that was happening to her. Why else would she be tying her shoes at the speed of light, all because she knew he was upset with her?

She scowled down at the offending shoes, and then sprang to her feet.

She was so tired of being confused by the man she could scream. All week, he'd treated her like his best friend's kid sister. No passes. No kisses. No touching. After that night at the restaurant, she'd expected . . . something. *Anything.* She'd have shut him down instantly if he'd pressed for an affair, but how could the man turn on like a deprived male animal on a dance floor and then not even try to hold her hand?

Had she suddenly developed the plague?

She viewed his stony face as she hurried out of her apartment wearing shoes and a sweater. A dozen turbulent emotions abruptly died. She hated the distant chill in his eyes and would have done cartwheels to erase it. "Where are we walking?" she asked peaceably.

"Anywhere."

Frustration made his answer terse. Without a word, he opened the outside door. Greer stepped out first. Cool darkness immediately enveloped them. Yellow yard lights illuminated sidewalks and reflected off long sweeps of glistening dark lawn. Night flowers and grass smells infused the darkness with a faint, inescapable sweetness, and stars hung low, hovering near a crescent moon. There was no one in sight, not even a car passing. The air was sweet and the silence soothing, but for a time Ryan noticed none of it.

The damn woman *wouldn't* let him help her. For an entire week, he hadn't laid a single finger on her. A *saint* would have been moved at the sight of Greer naked, but he'd managed to force himself to walk right out the door. What did it take to make her trust him? Her phone calls were one thing; he already knew he was going to take direct action where those were concerned.

But taking direct action with Greer was what mattered, all that mattered, and there Ryan felt lost. Irritable. Fighting a brick wall. What he wanted to do was simple. Kiss her senseless. Gather her up, protect her, love her, make love to her . . . but if he did that, he would risk losing her, he knew damn well.

His hands were jammed in his pockets. A delicate arm suddenly lightly wound itself through his and stayed there. He glanced down.

"This way," Greer said firmly. A germ of a rather insane idea had taken root in her mind.

They turned a corner and walked two more blocks. Greer again tugged slightly on Ryan's arm at the parking lot of the small brick elementary school.

"What on earth are you—"

"Just let me take the lead for once, McCullough."

His smile was half distracted, half exasperated, but it was still a smile. Greer grinned back, and then suddenly chuckled. Life wasn't simple. Nothing was ever simple, but one could only toss problems around for so long. It was break time, and she was going to chase away Ryan's brooding scowl if it killed her.

"You're crazy!" he called after her.

"So? Race you, McCullough!"

The playground was deserted and the grass soaked with dew. The silver-painted swings, merry-go-round, slide, and jungle gym caught the moonlight. The swing creaked when Greer settled into it. She pushed off and swung her legs in the air. Her crisp businesslike skirt immediately fluttered up to her thighs. "Are you just going to stand there, or are you going to push me?"

He pushed her, thinking dryly that it was at least one way of getting his hands on her fanny. He pushed her so high that she shrieked, and when the swing came back down she was wantonly leaning her head back, the breeze tossing her hair, her kissable mouth open with laughter. Now, how was he supposed to sustain his glum mood under those circumstances?

After that, she insisted on pushing him, and then she ran over to the slide, insisting he do the honors first. He did, but the slide was like glass, and the first time down he ended up on his seat in the sand.

Greer bent over him, shaking her head. "You need me to show you how it's done?" She barely missed a swat on her backside as she hurried up the metal ladder. At the top, though, she balked. "I'll wreck my skirt," she complained.

Ryan, still dusting off his jeans, roared, "Hike it up. You started this."

True. She climbed the metal ladder, pulled her skirt up, closed her eyes, and slid down on her slip. At the bottom, she gracefully sprang to her feet. "Nothing to it," she announced.

He chased her in and around the jungle gym and swings. She could hear her own laughter ringing out in the darkness, then his. There was no possible harm. The night was wonderful, warm and sweet. Greer mimed a batter's swing at home plate on the baseball diamond; Ryan mimed an imaginary pitcher on the mound. He was far better than she was. When he chewed an imaginary wad of tobacco and scratched his crotch, she collapsed in laughter, knowing exactly which major league pitcher he was imitating. After that, Ryan hooked an arm around her shoulders as they left the diamond.

"Ready for home?" she said breathlessly.

"No way." They were never leaving, if he had his choice. He'd never heard Greer laugh so freely, and there wasn't another woman on earth he could have shared so much nonsense with.

"Well . . . the merry-go-round then. We haven't done that." She reached the merry-go-round and tugged off her shoes. "Can't do this right unless you're barefoot," she called out to him.

"Can't you?" He couldn't stop looking at her. Her hair was wind-tossed, her eyes sparkling. A button had worked loose at the neckline of her blouse; she'd tossed off her sweater and pushed up the blouse sleeves. For once, she was unconscious of her body, and her movements were as free and spontaneous as they were sensual and natural. She was a seductress with a dirt spot on her seat. A Romany Gypsy, acting on impulse, the look and sound of her like magic.

She was Greer. The lady who'd started this madness to shake him from a bad mood, he knew. A lady he could play with as well as talk to. A lady he loved.

She bent over to start pushing the contraption around. He moved behind her, pushing in rhythm as she did until the merry-go-round picked up momentum. "Hop on," he ordered.

She did, clinging to the metal rails for support. "Too fast," she protested.

"I haven't even gotten it going."

They seemed to be spinning at the speed of sound. Her stomach was turning over at the same dizzying tempo. "You're crazier than I am. Would you *please—*"

"Just lie down and close your eyes and enjoy."

He vaulted up to her a second later. Flat on her back, holding on for dear life, Greer was conscious of the cold, hard metal beneath her, but not very. So fast . . . air rushed past, and darkness, and the silent houses in the distance. Exhilaration raised color in her cheeks, a smile that wouldn't stop. She turned her head to look at him.

The mad whirl stopped, or maybe it didn't. Maybe it even accelerated, and then something changed. Ryan reached out a hand, and it seemed utterly natural for Greer to take it. She let go of the metal bars, and suddenly he was holding her. More than holding her.

His legs were braced for balance, but his arms were free to both claim and secure. He hadn't planned that. He hadn't planned anything, but when he found her face that close, his mouth couldn't help but cover hers. Around and around and around . . . that rush of speed was hypnotic, as intoxicating as the rush of sensations that swamped him. The warmth and suppleness of her body, molding itself willingly to his. The crush of her breasts against his chest, the beat of her heart, the softness of her features in the whirling moonlight. His lips locked with hers, and he couldn't let her go.

Greer closed her eyes and hung on. She felt crazy, vibrant, high. Maybe there was no other gravity but Ryan. For that instant, she didn't know or care. With no one to push it, the merry-go-round gradually wound down, but her heart still spun with a kaleidoscope of sensations. The rush was so unexpected, so lush, so . . . easy. The feel of his warm, mobile flesh beneath her fingers. His thigh locked against hers. The sweet, intoxicating taste that was Ryan.

She wanted . . . something. So much. Something as exhilarating and delicious as their mad ride, something that Ryan's mouth was promising her, something his hands were promising in their rough sweep over her soft curves. His palm claimed her breast, cupping it, kneading, and she felt her heart quicken, heat gush through her veins.

*"Hey.* You kids. I've told you a thousand times not to use this playground as a necking park. Skedaddle, hear me? And next time I see you here I'm taking you home to your parents myse—"

Ryan placed a hand over Greer's mouth to muffle her startled cry. Disoriented, he raised his head. The police car was idling at the edge of the parking lot in the shadows, a window rolled down and a weary-looking gray-haired officer leaning out of it. Ryan's voice was strangled, but he managed a reasonably adolescent "Yes, sir."

"I mean it. You know what time it is? Gull dern kids."

As soon as they made to move, the patrol car drove off. Mortified, Greer leaped to her feet. For a minute, she was so busy gathering up her shoes, fixing her blouse, and pushing down her skirt that she couldn't possibly find time to look Ryan in the eye.

He didn't force it. For one thing, his body didn't want to do all that fast a recovery from the potent emotions Greer had aroused. For another, he was having a hard time believing he'd damn near made love to her on a children's playground. And for another, he wanted to savor that delicious uninhibited response he'd won from the violently flushing lady next to him.

And then, there was that policeman's bored face.

By her choice, they walked at a killing pace for two blocks before Ryan stopped, threw both arms around her shoulders, and bent his forehead to hers. His whole body was shaking with laughter. "You realize if he'd known we were adults we'd probably be en route to a mental hospital right now?"

"Do *you* realize we could have run into half the teen-agers in the county? That was obviously his nightly pa-trolling spot."

"You sure can pick the places, Greer."

Her body told her to be tense, to worry about how he would interpret her moments of craziness. Her heart just wouldn't listen to her body. She dissolved in laughter to match his. *"Me?* The walk was your idea." She added, "Haven't you ever gone down a slide, McCullough?"

"You're not going to let me live that down, are you?"

"I really don't think so."

They chuckled the rest of the way back to the apart-ment, but Greer unconsciously winced when they entered the brightly lit hall. Like a shout of reality, her knitting was still strewn on the floor, and so was his chess set.

Ryan didn't seem to feel the same effect. Yawning, he bent over to pick up her knitting and pile it in her hands, then stuffed his chess set back into its box and tucked it under his arm. "Pair of derelicts live here," he commented.

"Messy. Irresponsible."

"Tomorrow these irresponsible derelicts are going to spend a day on Cape Hatteras." He pushed open her door, and then leaned across their loaded arms to lay a swift kiss on her mouth. "No arguments."

She must have caught the determined note in his voice, because her eyes suddenly met his, as vulnerable as a cat's. He shook his head. He wasn't letting her shut herself up again in that independent world of hers. "We're going." And if she looked at him like that for one more minute he was going to toss both their stuff on the ground and swing her into a bedroom. Hers or his, it didn't much matter.

"I can't, Ryan. I have to meet with one of the men at work tomorrow," she said hesitantly, and gave him an apologetic look. "You see, Ray and I are both committed to attending a trade show next Wednesday and Thursday, and I promised him tomorrow—"

"Overnight?"

"Pardon?"

"You're going to a two-day trade show with this guy, you just said. Do you intend to stay overnight?"

She shook her head ruefully. "I'll be as safe with him as I would be in church," she said wryly, "so don't start up on potential callers again. Ray's specialty is coast-to-coast women; he wouldn't have time to make idle calls. Anyway..." She frowned thoughtfully, and took a long uneven breath. "I believe we'll be done by noon tomorrow. We're meeting early."

"Noon, then," Ryan said firmly.

Actually, she was done by ten. Her meeting with Ray went so smoothly she could barely believe it was over.

You've misjudged Ray terribly, she thought absently as she drove home under a sweltering sun. There hadn't been a soul at Love Lace that morning, no hum of sewing machines, no buzz of laughter and conversation. The downstairs offices had been cool, silent, and shadowed, almost like eerie tombs, ghostly with only the one light in the back office where they'd been working.

She'd been apprehensive, maybe because of the mood of the place, maybe because any confrontation with Ray aroused apprehension. Instead, Ray had made jokes; he'd been supportive; he'd waxed enthusiastic over practically every idea she had. She felt as if she'd spent the morning with Jekyll instead of Hyde.

The trick, Greer decided, was to work alone with him, away from other people. And to ignore the way his eyes kept . . . pinning her with those secret, enigmatic looks.

Egotism's your problem, not his, she scolded herself. Wry humor shimmered in her eyes as she glanced in the rearview mirror. A wonderful humor that she'd had since she woke up that morning. So being around Ray always disturbed her, but how egotistical was that? Just because a man looked at her sideways didn't mean he was a threat to her. Maybe if she worked alone with him more often, those reactions would go away. And he'd suggested a half-dozen more private projects in the future . . .

Ray dropped easily from her mind as she arrived home and flew into her bedroom. An entire day of play lay ahead of her, a treat she had every intention of savoring. Her feelings for Ryan last night had bubbled over into today. *When* had she ever laughed so much? She couldn't let it go. A little voice in her head was nagging frantically about combustible chemistry, but she ignored it. She refused to let *anything* ruin a perfectly good day.

Her swimsuit was buried deep, for good reason. A reason she ignored as she drew it out of the drawer and slipped it on with a grin. The suit was another of Love Lace's rejects, but this one wasn't too dreadfully flawed. It was a black two-piece suit with a modest halter top. The bottom was cut high on the thigh, only an eensy bit higher on one thigh than the other—enough for Marie to reject it, not enough so anyone else would notice.

Over the suit she pulled on a lemon-yellow terry-cloth top and navy shorts, then donned sneakers and a lemon and navy scarf. She fed Truce, stuffed a towel into a beach bag, threw open the door to her apartment, and stopped dead.

Ryan was standing there, leaning negligently against the doorjamb as if he'd been waiting in that same spot for four and a half years. His long body was casually attired in white jeans and a loose short-sleeved black shirt, open at the collar. His grin, impossibly, was both lazy and impatient. "Your meeting go okay?"

"Yes. Fine," she said, bewildered.

"*Exactly* okay? The dude didn't give you any trouble?"

"Ryan. Of course not. For heaven's sa—"

"Good. Let's go find my ocean," he said.

If she didn't need a keeper, why did he seem to have the job?

# Chapter Seven

"*YOUR* OCEAN?" GREER repeated with amusement some hours later, as they were driving down the central—and only—road along the Cape Hatteras National Seashore.

"All right, all right, you can claim a little shoreline." Ryan shot her a grin.

"That sounded grudging."

"I grew up believing the Atlantic was mine. Your coastline may be a little different from Maine's, but I'd still swear that's my baby."

"Possessive about the little things, aren't you?" Greer made one more vain attempt to adjust her scarf so the offshore wind wouldn't blow the hair into her eyes. Giving up, she pulled the thing off and tossed it on the dashboard.

"Better," Ryan approved.

*"You'd* think so. I can't see."

"Irrelevant. You look more like a sexy mermaid with your hair going every which way and the sea behind you."

Greer shook her head in despair. "No one's ever accused me of having scaly legs before."

She had to shout. When they'd reached the coast, Ryan had opened all the windows, liberally applied his foot to the accelerator, and turned up the radio. Barry Manilow claimed he couldn't smile without them. Greer had always been a sucker for Manilow's love songs.

And she was getting a glimpse of a very different Ryan today. His lazy grin never stopped; he clearly wasn't going to allow a serious thought to surface; and he was radiating a Huck-Finn-playing-hooky kind of charm.

Scrub-covered sand dunes whipped past them, bordering the road on both sides. Every once in a while they drove over a low hill and suddenly caught a glimpse of endless gray-green waters and foaming breakers. A puckish wind gathered enough momentum to push the clouds to someone else's horizon; other than that, the day was impossibly calm.

For Greer, work, people, and crank callers had disappeared. And McCullough, she thought dismally, was very badly under her skin—and getting worse. Few people could drag her near the water these days, and yet she hadn't hesitated to accept the invitation from Ryan, and worse, she had enjoyed every minute of it.

". . . didn't even live that close to the water, but close enough. It was never sufficiently warm for swimming—but we swam anyway. And we caught hake and trapped lobsters and any other sea creatures stupid enough to

come near a half-dozen noisy kids..." Ryan threw up
a hand at her patient-saint expression. "All right. All
right. I've been talking too much. You can have your
turn."

"I just thought I'd point out that the North Carolina
coast has a few goodies to offer that you Maine derelicts
never heard of."

"I doubt that."

"*My* ocean," Greer said firmly, "has got it all over
yours. For one thing, there've been zillions of ship-
wrecks. You can hardly walk the sands anywhere around
here without coming across a relic or two, memories of
lost treasures and history. This whole coast was famous
for its pirates, you know."

"Which is why you're dragging me all the way down
to Okracoke Island, when we could have stopped *anywhere* for the last hour?"

"Hush," Greer roared, and then mildly continued,
"Okracoke is sacred. Blackbeard's old lair. Although I'm
convinced that as a group the pirates were terribly misunderstood."

Ryan burst out laughing.

"What's so funny?"

"You. And misunderstood pirates."

"They *were*."

"Only to you, Brown Eyes."

She was about to explain indignantly, but didn't immediately have the time. Within fifteen minutes, they
were on the small ferry to the island, cars packed in front
of and behind them. The little white boat curled and
veered around endless channel markers, reminders of just
how treacherous these shallow inlet waters could be.

But treacherous was hardly the mood of the day. Greer's
senses were busy, soaking in the flavor of the windswept,

sun-drenched waters. Islands no bigger than a minute popped up from nowhere, coated with so many terns and gulls you couldn't see the sand. The mood was wild and free. A hot breeze came and went, and the air smelled fresh, sharp, and as if exhilaration were a component of the oxygen. Greer smiled, and kept on smiling as Ryan carefully drove off the ferry a few minutes later and then zoomed inland.

From the look of it, the ancient village of Okracoke might not have changed in three hundred years. The harbor was chock-full of swaying, paint-peeling boats; nets and buckets were strewn on the wooden walkways, and houses clustered close to the water, all watched over in benevolent silence by a tall white lighthouse. In minutes, they were past the town, and suddenly there was nothing. A sand-swept road without people or houses, and endless green waters beckoning on both sides of them, inviting them to enjoy.

Ryan pulled the car off the road and stopped. They paused thirty seconds to look at each other and then moved. They tossed their shoes in the back; shucked off their clothes; grabbed towels; and the race for the water didn't stop until their bare feet touched sand. Then, obviously, they had to dig their toes into the sun-warmed sand and savor a little.

Ryan draped an arm loosely around Greer's shoulder, and they wandered at a much lazier pace to the water. Waves were thundering in, scooping up fistfuls of sand and hurling them back into the depths. Beyond the breakers was a submerged sandbar, the covering blanket of water pale green in the sunlight, barely wrinkled from the touch of the breeze.

"Nice?" Ryan demanded.

"Nice," Greer agreed.

They walked. Shells speckled the high-tide line, sprinkling the sand with mauve and blue and sun-bleached white. Driftwood was scattered everywhere, sometimes in gnarled shapes that almost looked like people, but there was no one else around. High on the dunes, wild grape and sea oats waved sporadically, less to a wind than in the rhythm of the day.

In sheer laziness, they finally collapsed on the sand, utterly content simply to close their eyes and relax. The sun's rays soaked into their skin like warm magic, not too hot. The sun wouldn't have dared be too hot. Obviously, this was their beach, their sun, their day.

Not until then had Greer really been physically conscious of Ryan, of his long brown body and the bareness of it. His swimming trunks were relics, frayed, and once blue. They didn't cover much. He had a walker's legs, his thighs angular, distinctly male. His chest was smooth and gold, his small male nipples flat and dark. There was softness to his skin, but not to his body.

She was aware that she'd chosen the wrong swimsuit to wear around him. Perhaps, though, no swimsuit had been invented that was safe to wear around Ryan. Too quickly, his eyes had darted from her right thigh to the left, catching that minuscule error in Marie's design . . . only leaving Greer feeling that he didn' find it an error at all. She lay on her back with her eyes closed and tried to ignore that building physical awareness, but it was difficult.

He was slowly, intently pouring sand around her navel and then brushing it off. "You promised me some history," he accused. "I don't see anything that looks anything like Blackbeard's lair. In fact, there's nothing here at all."

Greer opened one eye. "That's the problem with you

Maine people. No imagination. We're sitting right in the middle of his living room."

"Ah." Ryan leaned back and threw an arm over his eyes with a contented sigh. "It's coming to me, slowly. The spirit of plunder and pillage."

Greer chuckled. "You were born with that, Mc-Cullough."

He squinted open one eye. "There isn't a soul around. I'd watch what you say, if I were you."

"Are you going to listen to me tell about the pirates or just continue to harass me?"

"If I have my choice—"

"You don't."

"I'm listening."

"All these coves and inlets made ideal pirate hideouts. The cargo ships had deep hulls that grounded in shallow water, where the pirates had cutters, swift and maneuverable anywhere. They could hide easily, ducking into the inlets, or they could chase a cargo ship into unfamiliar waters. Diamond Shoals, for example . . ." *Touch him, Greer.* The impulse surged through her like a wanton breeze that didn't want to settle down. His eyes were closed. His navel was an innie. She loved navels that were innies. There were specks of sand on his chest that needed brushing away. His skin was sun-warmed; she wanted to feel it.

"Are we getting to the misunderstood pirates yet?"

"Yes, you patronizing oaf."

She was afraid. She'd been afraid from the instant she'd met him. He was a boldly sexual man, different from any man she'd been close to, and the vibrations were . . . wrong. But not at this instant. Just once, she kept thinking. Just once . . .

"Pirates have acquired this terribly unfair reputa-

tion," Greer continued absently. "Exactly that plunder-
and-pillage thing. I'm sure they were nasty enough on
the high seas, but when they got into town I've always
had the feeling they turned into genuine good guys. I'll
even bet the women lined up when a pirate ship came
in. Where else were the ladies going to get their tea and
sugar? And they would have been struck with broadcloth
and homespun cotton if the pirates hadn't brought in
taffetas and silks and laces. And the pirates would hardly
have risked alienating the coastal people. Who else would
they have sold their goodies to?"

Again, Ryan opened one lazy eye. "Perhaps the women
did line up when they saw a black flag flying. But just
maybe they wanted to get a good look at a romantic devil
with a black eye patch."

The breeze combed through her hair like the caress
of a lover. The sun beamed down, so warm, so soothing.
Something about the island was infectious. At least the
strangest fever seemed to be infecting Greer, because she
couldn't stop looking at Ryan. She couldn't stop wondering what his sun-warmed body would feel like close
to hers.

"Greer?"

"Some romance. Most of the pirates had scurvy, scars,
and VD. I figure even the most man-hungry woman alive
had to be pretty desperate," Greer said prosaically.

Ryan burst out laughing, and lifted his head to look
at her. "Hey," he said suddenly, his voice soft.

He felt it, the change in her. An openness, an alluring
wistfulness in her eyes, a spark of something free and
burning and yet wary. Her eyes shuttered closed just that
quickly.

She needed touching, his lady. Badly. And he so badly

wanted to touch her, but it hadn't proved that simple. Not from the instant she'd stripped down to that simple black swimsuit. It was modest, as two-piece suits went, but then he hadn't understood until he'd seen her naked that no swimsuit was ever going to look modest on Greer. Her breasts were high and firm and full, her skin satiny, her hips gently rounded, her legs long and beautifully shaped. Tantalizingly shaped. Woman. All of her was Eve, the tease of lush curves and softness.

He wasn't in the mood for a little touch. He craved all of her. And now.

Abruptly, he stood up and grabbed her hand. "In the water with you."

"Wait a—"

"Insto-pronto. We'll swim past the waves and have a race for the sandbar."

She tried to regain that lighthearted feeling they'd shared earlier, laughing with him as he tugged her unwilling body to the shore. "I forgot to tell you, you've only got a wader here. No marathon swimmer. Ryan. Wait—"

"No waiting." His voice was teasing, yet it carried an undertone of tension. He needed, *now,* to get cool.

Water splashed and surged around her bare ankles, and Greer stiffened. "Ryan—"

"It's not that far. No more nonsense, woman."

"I don't swim."

His jaw dropped along with his hand. "You *what?* You live this close to the ocean and you don't—"

"Swim."

"I used to be able to," Greer said uneasily less than an hour later as she stared down into a placid aquamarine swimming pool. "As a kid, I was even into fancy diving. And that's exactly where I got into trouble. I was doing a double back-flip off the board—"

"*In,*" Ryan said firmly from the waist-deep water in the shallow end. He stretched out both arms to reach her, his fingers motioning impatiently.

"And I moved wrong, hitting the water on my back. I konked out—it must have been only seconds. When I woke up, I was underwater and I thought I was dead. Anyway. Ever since then—"

"*In.*"

She gave him a sour look. "What if I just plain completely change my mind about this?" she asked casually.

"Then we'll go home, foolish one. Obviously. But an hour ago, you were embarrassed as hell that you couldn't swim. Of course, the ocean's not the place to teach anyone to swim, but this will do beautifully." He motioned impatiently to her again.

"I would just like to discuss this a little longer."

"You've been discussing it for over fifteen years. The lady should have known enough to get back on the bike after she fell off."

"I *got* on the damn bike after I fell off," she said dryly. "This is different."

"It is not."

"It is. Oh, hell." She could have delivered a long dissertation about how the reaction of teenage boys to her figure in a swimsuit had been another reason why she'd never developed her swimming talents, but she didn't. She could never have told Ryan that; she'd never shared those embarrassing moments with anyone.

She slid her legs into the pool and then jumped, feeling the cool, clear water immediately rush and enclose her flesh to her ribs, but no higher. She dipped down, just to where her breasts would be modestly covered by water. She'd forgotten how delicious that feeling of weight-lessness was.

The other resort guests should have been enjoying the pool, but most of them were sitting in lawn chairs ab-sorbing the sun. Greer was totally unfamiliar with the resort. Ryan had stopped on the cape at the first place with a pool. The owners had accepted a bill from him for their right to use it.

The man could move incredibly fast when he was in the mood. And at the moment, his arms very swiftly, protectively enclosed her. She shivered free from that touch, staring at the droplets of water on his chest. And then up to his face. His hair was slicked back, wet from his dive, and for some reason his eyes looked bluer right now. Endless blue, a captivating sky blue. And those eyes wouldn't let her alone.

"This is silly, you know," she said with an embarrassed laugh. "First of all, I'm fine in the shallow end, and it's not as if I don't remember the strokes. I really *did* know how to swim once."

"Feel comfortable enough to prove it?"

"Of course." She raced him the width of the shallow end and then again, and then again. She was rusty and slower than molasses and increasingly annoyed with her-self. One really *didn't* forget how to swim. And it had been so long . . . she'd forgotten how deliciously buoyant water was, what it felt like to slice through that smooth coolness and just savor the sensuality of the water. On the last lap, because it was the only possible way to beat him, she dipped her head under, felt a moment's uncertain panic, and swam the last of it underwater.

She should have known she couldn't win. He was grinning, languidly relaxed with his arms outstretched at his sides, when she surged up with water dripping in her hair and eyes. "Feel good?"

She nodded.

"Not scared?"

She brushed the hair away from her eyes and tugged up her suit straps. "I feel like a perfect idiot," she said lightly. "I won't even mention coward. It's too humiliating."

He immediately pushed off from the side of the pool, gliding next to her, his hands sliding to her waist. "You're a long way from a coward, Greer," he whispered. "I never thought that. You think you're the only person who's ever been afraid of something?"

"All right. What phobias have you got?" Greer obliged. She was certainly more than sick of her own at the moment.

"Mice."

*"Mice?"* Her eyes sparked with amusement.

He nodded solemnly, his sun-browned face inches from hers. "Can't stand 'em. I had a little argument with a black bear in the woods once, and weathered that fine. But give me a mouse running across the room and my machismo immediately shrivels up. So there."

"Mice are adorable," Greer mentioned. "I've always loved mice."

"And you love swimming. Just not in deep water, right, lady?"

He captured her waist in his hands. The water skimmed over her ribs, then her breasts, then her throat, as he propelled her closer to the deep end. And they hovered there, their faces above the water, Ryan's arms securely around her. Deep water. Damn deep water, Greer thought suddenly. She could feel the brand of every one of his fingers on her bare waist.

"You afraid of anything else?" she asked breathlessly.

Her senses were picketing her rational mind, having a strike for unfair deprivation. She'd never felt deprived before. It was just now. The way the tips of her breasts grazed his bare chest. The way his shoulders felt slippery beneath her arms. The way her legs had to fight against the water's special gravity, not to move toward his, not to let thighs touch thighs. The water no longer felt cool, but warm, silky, inviting.

Danger was a sultry, sun-warmed day, a sky so blue it hurt her eyes.

"Just a little deeper," Ryan coaxed. "Hold on now."

She held on. He didn't give her much choice. His hands slowly glided down her spine to her hips, lifting her, forcing her to wrap her legs around him for security. Security, on the other hand, was becoming an elusive commodity. Her pelvis was intimately cradled against his flat stomach, and her breathing suddenly wasn't normal.

"There must be something else you're afraid of besides mice," she said frantically.

He considered exactly how delicious it would be to make love to her in the pool, and then banished the fantasy before it went too far. "Sure. My dad's temper. I figure I'll still be afraid of it when I'm a hundred and three."

Greer's eyes worriedly studied his. "He wasn't . . . mean to you as a kid?"

"Mean, no. Mad a lot, certainly. I was a rambunctious kid. But my father's reprimands were all noise; he wouldn't hurt a flea. Of course, I didn't know that when I was young. I'd hear that roaring voice and shake in my boots. The last time I heard it, he was ticked at something *he'd* done wrong—and I still shook in my shoes. I was six inches taller than he was, but I still shook in my shoes."

She chuckled. "I'd like to see you shake just once," she said suspiciously, finding it hard to believe that a roaring father or a harmless mouse could upset this particular man's equilibrium.

"Can do," he murmured, and she stopped smiling. His hands loosened their hold on her bottom and her body was suddenly free, free to slide down the length of his. His mouth had gently dropped on hers before she realized they were in deep water, that his feet could touch bottom but hers couldn't.

Ryan had no intention of letting her drown. Not in water. In a slow, languid motion he crushed her mouth, felt her lips part beneath his, and gently, coaxingly touched tongues with her. If there had been an audience of millions, he wouldn't have much cared.

Above the water, Greer could hear laughter, from a thousand miles away. And the sound of children cavorting in the babies' wading pool. And a roaring in her ears that might have been the distant ocean. Ryan's kisses were gentle, coaxing, layered one after the other until her lips felt swollen and overwarm and trembling. But that was above the water.

Below, she could feel the hardness of him pressed against her. His hands possessive on her hips and thighs. The heat of his body, an honest primal heat that he made no effort to hide from her.

He wouldn't hide. And Greer had never thought of herself as hiding from emotions; she was simply an expert at controlling them, at taming those rare unruly feelings that had no place in her life. All five senses seemed to be working against her today. Her heart refused to listen to her head. Her arms tightened around Ryan's neck, and her hips rubbed against his. She broke off from his kiss to bury her lips in his throat, and she clung to him, feeling the hot sun beating down, hearing his ragged breath.

She loved this man. She loved the way he made her laugh; she loved the way he protected her, and she even loved the way he challenged her. In a minute, she was going to feel frightened about the consequences of that love, but not yet.

"Greer?"

She kept her eyes closed, buried in the crook of his shoulder. "Unwise to start something like that in the middle of a crowded pool," she mentioned.

She heard the breath escape his lungs. "I want to make love with you."

"Yes."

"I've wanted to make love with you from the day I met you."

"Yes."

"But I'm *not* going to push you," he whispered.

"Yes, you are," she murmured. "Or I wouldn't be getting this feeling that you don't give a hoot in hell that a dozen people are watching us."

"I don't."

"I know that."

"Greer. *Stop* inviting." His hands clamped around on her slowly moving hips, to stop their seductive nudging against him.

"Why?"

"Because I need to be sure you really want this as much as I do."

"Do I actually have to scream yes in front of all these

people?" she teased softly. She felt his eyes searching hers. All she did was look back at him, but the next moment they were leaving the pool so fast she was breathless.

# Chapter Eight

RYAN AUTOMATICALLY LOCKED the door behind them.
His eyes skimmed the corner motel room, noting water-
blue carpet and furnishings, the small balcony where
draperies stirred restlessly from the ocean breeze, the
king-sized bed. He saw, yet paid little attention.

His eyes weren't about to leave Greer for very long.

She'd parted the drapes and flung open the glass doors
of the balcony the minute she stepped into the room.
Their silence was immediately broken by the distant crash
of surf, the faint scream of a gull on the beach.

They hadn't spoken during the short time it had taken
Ryan to check in or during the climb to their second-
floor room. He hadn't said anything because he couldn't.
Right or not, fair or not, he hadn't wanted to give her a

chance to change her mind. Knowing that grated against his conscience, but nothing could stop the pulse, the beat, the flow of desire he felt for her.

She turned from the balcony, her bare feet making no sound on the carpet as she stepped back into the room. Lashes shuttered her eyes, those beautiful, vulnerable, soft brown eyes...

Her hair had dried in soft wisps, and her face was in partial shadow, half as fragile as cream, half shaded a muted gold. The room had that dusty stillness of late afternoon. The feeling of life focused around Greer, the texture, look, scent of her.

She raised her eyes to his, and he heard the tiny sound of her breath catching. Her eyelids closed, then opened. Slowly, she reached behind her neck to undo the straps of her halter top. Ryan didn't breathe. The straps fell forward, revealing the smoothness of her neck and throat and a hint of swelling white flesh. She reached behind her again. The room was so silent he could hear the sound of her unlatching the clip at the back. The top fell, for a moment trailed in her hand, and then slipped to the floor.

Though her skin had long been sun dried, the suit had still been slightly damp. Her nipples were tiny, puckered, chilled. Her breasts were virgin white next to her tan, all smooth, firm flesh, impossibly soft. She stood tall, just slightly shivering, looking at him. He still couldn't move. He'd dreamed of her exactly like this, not just the nakedness but the beauty of her, the pride and softness, her sensuality, her vulnerability.

"Ryan—"

"Come here," he murmured, but he was the one to take the four steps to her. Taking her had been the only thing in his head moments before. That fierce primal desire hadn't diminished, but it had gentled. Now he reached out not to claim but to reverently touch, and not her body but her face.

The pads of his thumbs brushed along her cheekbones; his fingers whispered into her hair; he smoothed her eyebrows, traced the line of her chin. Her bare breasts were less than an inch from his chest; he didn't move that inch. He wanted all of her. But slowly. He didn't want to miss . . . anything.

Brown eyes met his. "Ryan? What's wrong?" she whispered.

"Nothing. Nothing at all, love." Did he look too grave? He smiled for her.

"There was, though. You were upset while you were checking in."

"A little."

"More than a little." The very smallest smile curled her lips. He hadn't realized until that instant that her smile had been missing. "You were about to belt the desk clerk when she looked around for our luggage. And you looked even more irritated when you signed in."

He drew in a breath, admitting quietly, "I hate motel rooms. And especially . . . for you. The woman said nothing. But if she'd even looked at you sideways—"

"You were afraid it bothered me, checking into a motel for the express purpose of making love?" She tilted her head, as if determined to see the hidden emotion in his eyes. "I think it's rather exciting, actually. Deliciously illicit. Wanton. All that stuff."

"All that stuff," he echoed faintly, and teasingly shook his head at her. She had the look of an innocent virgin testing out those words for the first time, but that wasn't what moved him. It was Greer, worrying about *his* feelings more than her own. "Go ahead," he whispered. "Tell me the place doesn't matter."

"The place doesn't matter."

"Nothing matters," he agreed, "except you."

His mouth lingered an inch from hers and then dropped, centimeter by centimeter, until his lips touched hers and sank in. To his surprise, she was suddenly trembling all over, and when her bare breasts grazed his chest, she breathed against his mouth in a hollow gasp.

He could feel her pulse quicken along with his own. Her skin warmed; so did his. She was already part of him. The only thing left was the claiming.

Blood beat in his throat in a steady dull throb. He discovered that her lower lip was irresistible. And that the shell of her ear could keep him entertained for hours. That her throat was softer than warm cream, that her nipples were infinitely sensitive to the slightest touch.

She kept trembling. Such fire . . . he'd never expected such fire. Where he wanted nothing more than to savor and linger over each new discovery, Greer was clearly impatient. He would have smiled, had there been time.

Her lips trailed feverish kisses over his face and neck. Her hips moved tantalizingly against him. When he stopped with ragged breath to look at her, she reached up for his mouth again. When his hands skimmed inside her suit bottom, she barely gave him the chance to take it off her before she pressed herself length to length to him, her eyes closed and her whole body still fiercely trembling.

He gathered her up, pushed back the bedspread, and placed her on the pillows. For one stark instant, he caught a glimpse of something dark and haunted underneath the sensual glaze in her eyes. Then she raised her arms, urging him down to her.

He dropped his suit and slid onto the bed next to her. She instantly enfolded his body, her hands feverish, her long legs curling invitingly around him. The male animal in him could no more have held back a response than stopped breathing, yet the speed with which she was asking to be taken was not what he wanted. For her. "Easy," he whispered. "Let me love you, Greer. Let me just . . . love you."

She went still so suddenly he almost smiled. With exquisite care he bent his head to the swell of her breast, capturing the small tight peak with the swirl of his tongue. Leaving it moist, he played with the other, while one hand stroked her flat stomach, learned the roundness of her hip more intimately. His lips trailed down to her navel, believed it virgin, and let his tongue do a lazy, thorough deflowering. Her skin . . . nothing had ever tasted as good as her skin.

His own was burning. He had never wanted a woman as much, but the process of knowing her this first time could easily have taken him years. He would not have guessed her nipples were so sensitive. He could not have known that she would tremble, that her eyes would take on such darkness, that her fingers would curl and uncurl on his skin . . . There were a thousand things he needed to know if he was to be a good lover for her. There was no way he could have known any of them ahead of time. Knowing a woman as a lover was different from knowing her in any other sense.

Every instinct told him to be careful, slow, gentle, because she was Greer, because she had taken a very long time to accept the love that was growing between them ... every instinct except that primal hardness pressed against her, which teased unmercifully when she writhed against him. And when his fingers slowly dipped between her thighs, Greer moved, her hands pushing him away, her pelvis cradling his in unmistakable demand. "Easy," he whispered.

*Easy?* Greer thought in despair. Suddenly nothing was easy. What had been natural and wonderful moments before was going desperately wrong. Still, she whispered, "Now, please, Ryan."

"Not yet..."

"Yes. Please. Please..."

She knew what he wanted. Every womanly instinct told her he wanted a seductress, an uninhibited lover who took and gave pleasure with ease. And for a while, she'd almost believed she could be that woman for him.

When they kissed in the pool, incredibly powerful emotions had surged through her. The feelings hadn't diminished when they'd come up to the room. When she removed her top, she'd felt proud of her body for once, proud to offer herself to him, glad that she felt no shame in wanting him.

Those emotions had been as real as the lush surge of desire she'd felt when bare skin had touched bare skin, as real as the love she felt for him. But old ghosts had intruded from nowhere. From an awareness that it had been a long time since she'd been with any man, that she might be awkward. From an awareness that the tepid sexual relationship she'd shared with her ex-husband was not the sort that Ryan would settle for, that he would not be fooled. And inside, deeper, she still bore the scars of an adolescent girl who'd fought the sexual side of her nature. She'd had to, to survive.

Her present sexual feelings were confused by the

memories. Greer had a sudden terrible need simply to be held, to explain, to tell him she needed to go slowly, that she was uncertain. But she couldn't ask that. Ryan would surely feel contempt for a twenty-seven-year-old woman who wanted only to be held.

She was trying so hard to be a cream-lace-on-pink-satin kind of woman, but she couldn't stop trembling. Pleasing him mattered so much. She loved him. Too much.

"Greer?"

She heard the question in his voice, but she could also feel the beat, the warmth of him pressed against her belly. "Now," she whispered. "Don't slow down, Ryan. Not for me. Please..."

She felt a slight hesitation in him and wound her arms tighter around him, whispering something, she didn't even know what. Her body arched, her fingers whispered over his skin. With a low groan, he slid into her, surging deep, filling the yawning hollow inside her.

Her eyes closed in sheer unexpected pleasure. For a moment, all the ghosts went away. He felt... wonderful. She felt different, the way she'd felt earlier in the pool, high on the touch of him, high on his warmth and those incredibly powerful surges she felt when she was near him. For the first time, she glimpsed something huge, special, secret, inextricably linked to the woman in her. Her body was about to burst from some elusive force that was just out of reach but so close...

"So beautiful," he murmured. "Your skin, your taste, the look of you. Come with me, Brown Eyes. Come with me..."

She wanted to. She so desperately wanted to. But she was also terribly afraid Ryan wanted something from her ... that just wasn't there.

* * *

The sun had gone down. Dusk filtered in. The tide splashed in the distance, a lazy, early evening tide, a lulling, rhythmic murmur that never ceased.

"Greer?"

She opened one sleepy eye.

"What on earth are you doing way over there?" Ryan inquired mildly. His voice was groggy with sleep.

He reached out one long arm and tugged her closer to his bare warmth. She didn't tell him that she'd assumed he would prefer no contact after lovemaking. Her ex-husband had always wanted to be left alone afterward.

Ryan had other ideas. He fussed with her arm until it was tucked under his waist, then lay down again and dropped a leg over her to bring her closer yet. She would have smiled at all his engineering, if she'd been less tense. As it was, she made her body go languid . . . and that wasn't so hard to do.

His chest was warm, his hand soothing a caressing stroke up and down her back. Her cheek fit perfectly in the crook of his shoulder, and she sighed, not able to stop loving the warmth of his arms around her. Not trying.

"Are you going to tell me what all that was about?" he whispered lightly.

"Pardon?" her eyes blinked open on the vein in his neck.

"I was just curious about whom I was making love to." He leaned over to press a kiss, first on her forehead, then on her nose. Blue—grave blue—eyes focused on her startled brown ones, though there was a faint, even gentle, smile on his lips. "You worked very hard to cheat yourself," he whispered. "I've been trying to figure out why for an hour, and I can't. You're going to have to give me a clue."

"I don't—what are you talking about?"

He said nothing, just continued to press another series of kisses down the side of her face, into her neck. When she stiffened, his arm tightened. Except for that, his touch was petal soft.

"You weren't . . . pleased?" she whispered hesitantly. "Ryan, it's been a long time since I—"

"I know that." He raised himself up on one elbow and started stroking her hair back from her forehead, over and over. "Would you look at me?" he whispered.

Her lashes fluttered open.

"You're my Greer again," he murmured. *"Now* you're my Greer again. A little shy, though you don't like anyone to know that. Sensual as a kitten who wants to curl up in the sun. And certain things . . . certain things were you, weren't they, Brown Eyes? Your breasts are extremely sensitive. You like the lightest touch. And you're a born hedonist, my lady. You like to be rubbed; you like the feel of skin against skin. No. Open your eyes."

His tone was light, but she obeyed him because there was something else in his voice as well.

*"I* failed *you,* Brown Eyes. Not the other way around," he said quietly. "Pretending isn't the way, though, honey. What bothers me is that you felt you needed to."

She suddenly couldn't possibly meet his eyes. "I don't know what you mean," she said lightly, slipping out of his arms, trying not to hurry, trying to ease away from him as if the only thought in her head was to take a languid stretch after lying still so long. "I'm starving," she announced. "Do you realize what time it must be? And it's getting cold."

She crossed the room to push the balcony doors closed. Her heart was trying to trip over itself. Ryan was silent behind her, at least for a moment.

"I'll order up a meal," he said finally. "Since you're suddenly that hungry."

"No." She turned to him with a brilliant smile and then reached rapidly for her swimsuit. "I have to go home."

"No, you don't. Tomorrow's Sunday. We can stay all of tonight and tomorrow as well."

"The cat," Greer said regretfully. "I can't leave him, Ryan. There's no one to feed him. Really, I have to go home."

She slipped on the bottom of her swimsuit, then turned away as she put on the halter, her fingers all thumbs, slippery, clumsy. Only when she was covered again did she steal another look at Ryan.

He was still lying there on the bed. One of his legs was bent at the knee, he'd pushed both pillows behind his head, and he appeared as unaware of his nakedness as she was of how naked she suddenly felt. His eyes were on hers, spears of blue that pierced her skin, her mind, her heart. He was trying to guess . . . things. Things she didn't want him to know.

Had he found her wanting? *Did* he find her wanting? And if he did, that was nothing less than what she should have expected. Greer felt a sudden disastrous urge to cry. Not a tear here and there, but a burst of them.

Slowly, Ryan sat up, and then stood, still watching her. She was acting as if this were a one-night stand, for which he would have shaken her . . . if she'd been anyone but Greer. Greer was an irrational, damnably incomprehensible, totally illogical woman, but he could sense that she was ready to burst into tears and that to push her was to risk losing her.

He considered slamming his fist into the wall, and put

on his swimming trunks instead. He didn't have the least idea what had gone wrong for her. Maybe it was the motel. Maybe it was too soon. Her ex-husband?

It was there, between them. Wanting. Love. Caring. All of the things that mattered. Ryan would have slain dragons for her, but Greer didn't let anyone slay her dragons for her.

They drove home in silence, stopping for hamburgers along the way. Greer curled up on the seat next to him, wrapped in a towel as if she were cold, even though the night air was muggy and he was waiting—*needing*—to reach out and hold her. Halfway home, he gave in to the blasted impulse, reached an arm around her shoulder, and tugged.

She settled willingly with her head on his shoulder for the rest of the ride. Whatever her emotional state of mind, the tension in her body gradually dissolved. He flicked on a Manilow tape, because she'd clearly liked Manilow. He played it low, and over the miles felt her body ultimately relax in sheer exhausted sleep.

At home, he switched off the ignition and sat in the car holding her. His arm was stiff, folded around her. He wanted to leave it there. The night was pitch dark except for the apartment's floodlight. A ray zigzagged across Greer's cheek, her shoulder, one bare white breast that her swimming top couldn't hide, not in that position. Desire stirred in him, a deep, powerful desire to make love to her again.

And a second time she wouldn't get away with pretending. A second time he would send her over the edge, whether she wanted it or not. A second time he'd listen to his own instincts, not to the messages she sent him. He wasn't a psychologist and didn't want to be. He cared less why Greer had behaved the way she had than that he'd been blind enough to let it happen, when he'd wanted to ensure that their lovemaking was good for her. There would be a second time. Earthquakes and hurricanes wouldn't stop there being a second time.

But not, unfortunately, this evening. He opened the car door. She murmured. He got out first, still leaning over to hold her so she wouldn't fall, and then lifted her legs out, snaking his arms around her waist.

"Did I fall asleep?" she murmured groggily.

"No." For the first time in hours, he smiled. Greer was limp lettuce, draped over his shoulders, her bare toes grazing the ground and her eyes still closed. Ryan slammed the car door. "Where's your key, love?"

"Flowerpot."

"Pardon?"

She waved an arm in the general direction of the moon. "Flowerpot."

He gathered she kept an apartment key in that wrought-iron urn in the hall. He'd figured out a while back that it was her urn and geraniums anyway. And if he'd known she'd pick such an obvious place to put a spare apartment key, he would probably have throttled her.

It didn't seem the time. She kissed his neck as he walked in. Both of her arms stayed loosely draped around him. Her feet marginally obeyed the learned impulse to walk. He simply lifted her up the steps.

"I'm awake," she announced again at the door.

"Good," he murmured as he opened it, keeping her propped up with his other arm. "Because we're about to have a small discussion, Greer."

The cat leaped at them in the dark, meowing furiously. Ryan switched on a light, nearly dropped his leggy bundle in the process, and with a sigh, picked Greer up in his arms.

"Truce," she murmured. "Hungry."

"And since we're having this complicated intellectual discussion," Ryan whispered, making his way with her through the dark hallway, "I thought I'd mention that I've taken over your crank caller, sweet. All arguments are worthless. Don't bother."

"Mmm."

He meant to place her gently on the bed. It ended up as more of a flop than a gentle laying down, but Greer didn't seem to mind. The faint light from the living room was enough, once his pupils adjusted to the dark. "I thought you'd see it my way," he whispered soothingly, as he tenderly peeled off her swimsuit. "You've been afraid too long, Greer. And you've had reason to know fear in these last months. But I'll be damned if you're going to be afraid of *me*. And I'll be doubly damned before I sit still and watch you take on the entire world alone again. And don't argue."

He sensed rather than saw her eyes blink open. "Ryan?"

"Go back to sleep."

"What are you do—"

He tossed the suit on the floor. Before she could blink, he'd folded her in her sheet and blanket. He hesitated then, his palm close to her cheek, the need to touch her one last time irresistible. His fingers trailed the line of her cheekbone, brushed into her hair. "You want me to stay, Greer?" he whispered.

There was silence. Amazing, how much physical hurt he could feel, just like that, just that sharp and searing.

His hand dropped and he straightened.

The cat was waiting for him in the hall. Swearing silently under his breath, he foraged in Greer's kitchen cupboards until he found the cat food, then filled Truce's dish. The cat attacked the first bite as if starved, looked up, and promptly wound himself around Ryan's legs with a thunderous purr.

Warmth clearly rated over hunger. Ryan petted the cat, crouched on Greer's kitchen floor in the semidarkness. At that moment, the feline struck him as remarkably like Greer. Greer, too, craved warmth, physical contact, touch, and affection. And denied the existence of hunger. The very natural hunger that was an extension of affection, as natural as breathing.

The cat wasn't interested in his comparison. For fifteen minutes, Ryan stroked Truce, until he was finally sated enough to bounce soundlessly back to the food bowl, purring like a Mercedes. Ryan straightened. "Why do I get the impression that you'll be on the foot of her bed within five minutes of my leaving here?" he murmured dryly, and then moved toward the door.

He spotted the phone en route, silently took it off its hook, and placed a couch pillow over it. The cat, fool that it was, followed him. "Go back and eat," he ordered it quietly, "and then you go right ahead and sleep with Greer. I'm warning you now, though, that your days are numbered."

The cat didn't seem impressed.

He let himself out of the apartment, crossed the hall, and stuck a key in his own lock. "I'm talking to cats now," he muttered dourly. "That woman has a lot to answer for."

*Soon,* his mind echoed silently.

# Chapter Nine

*"GREER?"*

Marie's high-pitched voice caught Greer in midstride. She backed up two paces to the open door of the finishing room. Marie frantically motioned her inside.

"I've been waiting to catch you all day. I want to show you something."

It was that kind of Monday. All day Greer had tried to hide behind her desk with a good solid dose of depression, but the outside world just wouldn't give her time. Impatiently, she followed Marie past the steady hum of sewing machines, into the small spotless room beyond, where the garments were stored. Marie stood on tiptoe and took a garment from a hanger, laying it over her arms for Greer's inspection.

"What do you think?"

Greer shifted the papers in her arms to a nearby chair, dropped her glasses to her nose, and delicately fingered the sparkling material. The shift was long and sleek, with dolman sleeves and a high side slit. "Not lamé?" she questioned.

"Of course not lamé. A metallic acetate; it cleans like a dream. Of course, it is a bit wicked..."

"Decadent," Greer murmured dryly.

"Maybe a little too 'thirties.'"

"It's very thirties," Greer agreed thoughtfully.

"You don't like it." Marie's voice fell.

Greer peeked over her glasses with a grin. "You know darn well it's fantastic. For the holidays. Is that what you had in mind?"

"Of course."

Greer again fingered the shiny material. "I think that's exactly how we should market it. 'Decadent. Wicked.' We can haul out the old spiel about feeling irresistibly sexy when completely covered from neck to toe..." She was murmuring to herself more than to Marie, until the other woman laughed.

"You *always* know exactly what I have in mind," she said triumphantly. "If you could only draw, you would be a great designer. Outstanding."

Greer looked slightly alarmed. "You're not going to start that again—"

"No, of course not. The last time I tried to show you the techniques of drawing, you gave me a migraine. You drew a breast the size of a nose. Your people looked like stick figures. Your—"

"Yes," Greer interrupted, chuckling, and handed the shift back to Marie. "You left a note on my desk this morning. Something about thread?"

Marie hung up the garment with loving fingers. "For the trade show, yes. I know today's only Monday, and you won't leave for two more days, but I wanted to ask you about Barteau."

Greer looked blank.

"He will be there. You will give him a kiss from me, and then you will steal every little tidbit of information you can. I want to know what he is up to. How much cotton is he using this year? How much finishing is he doing by hand? And most important, you must get his *thread*. Steal some, if you can. I hear he has found a new silk blend, a stronger fiber, but where he's getting it . . ."

"Steal some *thread?*" Greer echoed wryly.

"Now, don't get that *look*, darling. And keep in mind that Barteau will be probably peek under your skirts if you let him. He was a dirty old man even when I studied under him, and he was only in his twenties then. Now." Marie folded her arms over her chest as Greer picked up her folders. "We are all alone, not a soul here. What's wrong?"

Greer was halfway to the door, and turned. "There's nothing wrong."

"Of course there is. You didn't eat lunch; you barely said a word at the sales meeting this morning. Your eyes are sad. Something happened between Friday and today. A man?" Marie guessed.

"A bad case of no sleep." Greer was willing to admit to that.

"Fib."

"All problems are not caused by men," Greer suggested mildly.

"Only the problems worth having. The circles under your eyes are a positive sign. A good lover *should* make you tired. But not listless, *chérie*." Marie shook her head. "I can see from your face you do not want to talk. Fine, that is your business. But should you ever need an expert—"

Marie winked, her smile full of affection and humor, and for a moment Greer almost hesitated. Marie would listen, she knew. But Greer never burdened anyone else with her problems, and to discuss anything as personal as the touchy relationship between love and sex—never. She shook her head. "You're a sweetie. But there's nothing, really," she assured Marie, and they parted at the stairs.

In her office, Greer sank into her chair, slipped off her cream-colored sandals, and slid her glasses on top of her head. Depression promptly caved in on her like an avalanche. Never having catered much to the moody blues, she wasn't quite sure what to do with them. And today was merely an extension of the day before.

Sunday she'd wakened alone, mortified and lost as she recalled making love with Ryan. She'd taken her car and simply driven half the day, going nowhere, thinking nothing. By late afternoon, she returned, knowing she had to face him.

She'd found him in the back courtyard, barbecuing steaks. Two steaks. There seemed no question in his mind that she'd arrive on time to share them with him. He'd looked incredibly lazy and easy in cutoffs and a loose dark shirt; he'd dropped a kiss on her mouth the minute he saw her; he'd forced her to absolutely stuff herself full of steak, foil-cooked corn dripping in butter, and éclairs he'd picked up earlier at a bakery.

And when dinner was over, it was dark and the mosquitoes had started buzzing. Greer and Ryan had separated and gone to their respective apartments. There'd been a kiss that could have resurrected fire from dead ash, but Ryan hadn't pressed. He'd been warm, affectionate, and funny. Disastrously easy to be with. But he'd clearly expected to sleep alone that night.

Greer was not surprised.

Depressed, but not surprised. Absently, she plucked an imaginary speck of lint from her oyster-colored linen skirt and then stared at her outfit darkly. The oyster skirt, cocoa blouse, and pearls were old favorites, a choice based on past experience to pick up her mood. They were failing her.

She wasn't much of a lover. She was good at listening, and terrific at making pot pies; her empathy was laudable, and she was just plain excellent at her job. But she'd never been much of a lover.

Wearily, she touched her fingers to her temples, denting the skin white with unconscious pressure. She had *known* that, long before she got involved with Ryan. And she'd sensed up front that Ryan would be an exciting, imaginative, and experienced lover. Too experienced to be fooled by a lady trying to fake it.

He was the last man she should have let herself fall in love with.

"Looks to me like our resident sex symbol needs a drink."

Her head popped up to see Ray lounging in the doorway, the sleeves of his white linen shirt rolled up at the cuffs, his spotless black suit pants perfectly creased. His tone, as always, overflowed with husky seductiveness. And as always, it grated on Greer's nerves.

She could barely keep the impatience out of her voice. "I take it you got the figures back from the regional sales studies we did?"

He nodded. "But it looks to me as if you're much

more in a mood for a bottle of wine and a night of love than discussing midwestern sales patterns."

Greer reached out for the folder in his hand. "I'll settle for the statistics on girdle sales in Ohio, but thanks."

He dropped the file on her desk. "One of these days you're going to realize what you're missing."

"I'll survive," she assured him as she thumbed through the statistics he'd brought her. "Did I tell you this or did I tell you this? The Corn Belt's going nuts for negligees."

"Not exactly the Corn Belt, but close enough." Ray lowered himself into the chair by her desk, his lazy black eyes skimming over her figure in the cocoa blouse. He was a man who specialized in mentally stripping women; yet Greer had never figured out how his eyes could be so opaque, so unreadable. "I won't say I didn't resent Grant's pushing you into my marketing corner, but I have to admit you know your stuff. Now, southern women I would have guessed, but never that the farmers' wives would go for frills and lace."

"I've been telling you for ages that psychology and marketing shouldn't be strangers." Greer shoved her glasses onto her nose and flipped through the last pages of his report.

"And I've been trying to tell you exactly the same thing for months, darling."

"Pardon?" She lifted her head from the neatly typed pages distractedly.

"It's only a half-hour until quitting time. I was about to suggest a drink afterward."

For a moment, she couldn't think of a thing to say. For all his constant sexual patter, Ray had never asked her out before. The offer made her oddly nervous. "I really can't, not tonight. Maybe another time . . ."

"Why did I know you'd say that?" Ray's smile was

cool. He moved to the door, but then turned suddenly, that practiced smile gone from his face. "You know, I thought we'd made inroads this last week, working together. Obviously, I was mistaken."

She frowned. "I don't know what you're talking about."

"I think you do. I thought if we worked together a little more closely, you might just thaw out. Obviously not."

"Ray!" Greer fumbled for words. "I care very much that we work well together. I always have. But beyond that—"

"Beyond that, if any other man in the place had asked you for a drink, you would have gone."

Greer clamped her jaws together. "For heaven's sake. I've had a drink after work with Barney once in the five years I've worked here—"

He was gone. Bewildered, Greer shook her head. She'd never seen Ray behave so . . . ridiculously.

For the next half-hour, she pored over the regional statistics he'd brought her, and fretted over the confrontation. She'd always regarded him as an insensitive, chauvinistic s.o.b. Well, he was. But perhaps she herself had shown a lack of sensitivity toward his feelings. Had her dislike of him shown through?

The thought upset her. Simply because she didn't like the man didn't mean she wanted to hurt him. And she knew she *hadn't* made any serious efforts to understand Ray, as she had with the others at Love Lace. She hadn't cared enough to try.

Besides, one short drink after work wouldn't have hurt you, she scolded herself. For the first time since you've been here, he's actually trying to get along. You blew it.

Bodies were moving past her door. Greer glanced at

the clock and gathered up the report and her purse. Feeling utterly low, she made her way down the hall, anxious simply to be home where she could mope in peace. She was fumbling with sunglasses at the back door when she heard a sneeze.

Normally, a sneeze was hardly enough to make her turn around, but this one sounded out of place. Grant's office was behind her; she backed up three steps to where she could see through the windowed partition.

The office hadn't changed; it still had a teak desk so well polished you could use it for a mirror to put on lipstick, a neat array of bookshelves, and a wall collage of photographs—models in various styles of lingerie— that Greer could never fathom why Marie tolerated. The office was the same, and Grant was the same, his blue suit impeccable on his square, lean form, his mustache meticulously trimmed, his posture, as always, erect. The only thing out of place was Ryan.

Work boots, jeans, hard hat, sun-weathered skin . . . Ryan was a shout of sheer sexy machismo next to Grant's overmanicured smallness. The difference between the men was more than physical, Greer mused for a second and a half. Grant was the kind of man who would make lingerie. Ryan was the kind women wore it for.

That second and a half passed quickly, during which she was quickly striding the five steps necessary to walk inside Grant's door, where she stood, her jaws clamped into a counterfeit smile.

"Greer!" Grant leaned back on his desk, motioning her in. "I told Mr. McCullough you'd be passing by here any minute. I was just filling your friend in on the industry."

"Done for the day?" Ryan queried lightly.

She nodded. Ryan offered a hand to Grant, and the two men exchanged a few more pleasant words before Greer found herself escorted from the office into the hot sunlight of the parking lot. Just as Ryan's stride was lithe and easy, Greer's was stilted and clipped.

"You'd better be good for a ride home, honey. I was dropped off here."

"And just miraculously ran into my boss in the farthest office in the back?"

"Once I had the receptionist call him, yes."

*"Why?"* Greer asked, bewildered, as she climbed into the driver's seat and hurriedly rolled down the windows against the sweltering oven inside. Ryan folded up his knees next to her, tossed his hard hat in the back, and grinned. "McCullough, what are you up to?"

"Infiltrating the enemy lines."

"Fine. Where's the war?"

"Don't get nervous. I was swarmed the minute I walked in the back door. I never asked for all the attention."

"Most people use the front door."

"And face all that *stuff* in the window?"

Greer chuckled. "You mean underpants?"

He shoved down his visor against the relentless late afternoon sun. "Looked like a pretty decent group of people you work with."

"You'd figured them for flakes. Because of the lingerie," Greer said wryly.

"I hadn't figured them for anything at all. Don't jump to conclusions, sassy." He paused. "I must have met at least five of your colleagues." And there was no need to mention that he'd engineered all of those meetings. "There's no question they're fond of you."

"And I love them back," Greer said mildly.

"The first one I ran into was a man named Ray. The one you mentioned you'd be going to that trade show with."

"Hmmm." Traffic was thick, less because of rush hour, since Greenville really didn't have that much of a rush hour, than because of a muggy day when drivers were crabby.

"You trust him, Greer?"

"Ray?" She chuckled, darting around a poky Chevy. "No woman in her right mind would trust Ray." She flashed Ryan a glance. "I can land a mean right hook, if that's what you were thinking. And you work in an office yourself, so don't tell me there isn't a woman around who makes the men occasionally nervous. It comes with the business. You can't like everyone you work with, and some people are more aggressive than others."

"Yes." He wanted to pursue it, but didn't. Greer's voice held a defensive pride. *I can handle my own problems. I always have.* Ryan watched her steadily maneuver in and around the other cars. "Are you going to feed me tonight?" he asked casually.

"No." But she was. She had known the minute she saw him that she was doomed again. It wasn't wise, getting involved with McCullough; she had been foolish to sleep with him, and the best thing she could possibly do now was tactfully ease herself out of any further intimate contact. Besides that, she was hot, tired, and irritable; she had to call her mother ... and blood was dancing up and down her veins just from being this close to Ryan again.

"Greer? It's a red light."

Obviously. She turned to him quizzically as she stopped the car, unsure why he was stating the obvious. His face loomed closer, much closer. So swiftly, so softly, his lips

touched hers. And again. And then sank in the way a
pillow sank in, a soft crush of weight, leaving the molded
indentation of his mouth afterward. She was staring at
him, dark eyes bemused, confused, and warm with long-
ing, when the car behind her honked.

She jammed her foot on the accelerator. The car stalled.
Ryan chuckled.

"Listen," she began abruptly as she started the engine
and drove through the intersection.

"I'm listening."

But Greer didn't have anything to say. Ryan sneezed
again, and she frowned.

"Are you catching something?"

"I *never* catch *anything.*"

"What's wrong with your car?"

"Nothing. Just needed an oil change. And I used the
excuse to get dropped off where you'd be stuck taking
me home."

"Didn't it once occur to you to call? I might have
been working late."

"I considered that, rationally. Except that rational de-
cisions haven't always worked out too well lately."

"Pardon?"

At her apartment, a tall, towheaded boy was ambling
out of their building with a sack of newspapers slung
over his shoulder. He brightened at the sight of Greer.
"Hi." His voice sounded cracked and wistful.

"Hi, Johnny," she returned warmly. "Life treating you
okay?"

The boy spread his fingers and wagged his hand back
and forth, and Greer chuckled. "You're not alone," she
assured him as she waved good-bye and fumbled for her
apartment key.

Ryan glanced back, to see the boy staring at Greer—

at least until he caught Ryan's deadpan stare. Johnny turned in a hurry, flipped up the kickstand of his bike, and sped off. Ryan climbed the stairs at a more sedate pace, noting that Greer's newspaper had been neatly tucked behind her doorknob. His own had been haphazardly tossed near the mailbox.

"Known him long?" he asked.

"Who?"

"The kid."

Greer looked up. "Sure. Johnny and his mom have lived across the street for as long as I've been here."

"He's got a crush on you."

"Yes. Painful. On both sides. I wouldn't hurt him for anything; he's a sweetheart." She glanced up when Ryan stole the key from her hand and motioned her toward his place. "I thought you wanted me to cook?"

What he wanted her to be was *safe,* and away from every damn male but him.

Prepared for a touchy exercise in tact, Ryan had found her boss more than willing to listen. Grant clearly appreciated Greer's talents and was personally fond of her. Ryan had liked him instantly. The man had been disturbed that Greer hadn't mentioned her crank calls to him, and not all that quick to discount any of his employees as possible culprits. He wasn't in a hurry to malign any of his staff, but Grant admitted that several men would have done more than look at Greer if she'd ever given them the first encouragement. If Ryan was implying that those calls could mean a threat of a sexual nature . . .

Ryan had implied nothing. He'd said it straight out.

The police had assured him that nuisance callers rarely followed through on their telephone threats. Despite that, every instinct told him that this caller was a sexual threat to Greer.

And Ryan was disturbed, frustrated, fiercely protective, and beginning to worry about even fourteen-year-old boys who looked at her.

He coaxed. "You haven't seen my place since it was decorated in packing crates. We can eat there just as well."

"I need to change my clothes, my mother calls on Mondays, and I—"

"You can call her from my apartment, or vice versa. I had an extension of your phone installed this morning."

"You *what?*"

Greer's temper simmered helplessly while Ryan shoved some kind of gourmet TV fare in the oven, showed her around the apartment, nudged a dish of mixed raisins and nuts into her hand, and left her to muddle around while he disappeared to change his shirt.

By the time they finished dinner, she figured he had to have exhausted himself with inconsequential nonstop patter about engineering, and weather, and his mother's love of gardenias, and health care in England. Only after dinner, he installed her on the couch. His furniture was new; she couldn't help but approve of it. The couch was an off-white nubby affair, and she sank into it so deeply and so comfortably that she doubted she could get up.

Her stocking feet seemed to be propped on an ottoman, and she hadn't seen her shoes in an hour. It was tough, dredging up irritation when she was so comfortable. The rest of his new furnishings were equally pleasing. He had placed them all wrong—men will be men—but they were tasteful and appealing. Brass lamps, an oak rolltop desk, shelves in pecan, a coffee table in that rare dark marble she'd seen only in books before . . . The only thing he hadn't found a place for was a painting.

The oil was resting on the floor against the wall, a seascape at dawn; the creamy breakers were rolling in, and the waters beyond were a bright, endless blue. The blue of Ryan's eyes.

"That's been sitting there for days," he said casually. "Wouldn't have any ideas where I should hang it, would you?"

She had several ideas where Ryan was concerned, none of them mentionable. In a demonstration of totally out-of-character garrulousness, he'd mentioned lightly that he'd had a very busy day with the police and the phone company on her behalf. Now her phone—temporarily—rang in his apartment as well as her own. Since it was past time to get to the bottom of the caller mystery, he couldn't imagine that she had any objections.

Four times she'd opened her mouth to read him the riot act. Four times she'd closed it.

Confusion kept her silent. She heard Ryan's overt message, but she heard the unspoken one as well. She'd given him certain rights when she made love with him. Privacy and lovers didn't go together, of course. Or they shouldn't. When you loved someone, you bared your vulnerabilities, laid open your weaknesses. Like the things you were afraid of.

And where Greer could have criticized Ryan for interfering if he'd been a friend, she couldn't bring herself to do so now. He'd gone over her head only because she'd given him certain rights. To love. And in loving, to protect.

Ryan, so very subtly, was bulldozing her with the fact that he considered her part of his life.

He was also busy wandering to and from the other rooms. He placed a hammer in her lap. Then two nails. Then some wire. By the time he plopped into the chair across from her, he managed somehow to look boyishly innocent.

Greer sighed. "Why do I have the feeling you've never tried to hang a picture before?"

"I have. But they always end up crooked." He added hopefully, "Do you want a tape measure?"

"No. You can't do these things by measuring. You have to do them by the look of the thing."

She didn't want to do it. Putting up pictures was another one of those things. Those intimate things. It didn't involve naked skin, but it was still inescapably intimate. The picture had bothered her from the instant she'd walked in, not because it was on the floor, but because she wanted it in the right place. An idiotic feminine impulse. A desire to put her personal stamp on his place. An instinct that assumed a vested interest, and she didn't dare give in to it.

"I thought about hanging it over the TV," Ryan said absently.

"No!" The painting would look wretched there. Dammit. Feeling helpless, Greer stood up, straightening her blouse, and surveyed the picture and the room with a critical eye. "You *can't* put it there. Hang it over the couch or on that wall so you can see it when you come in..." Her eye lingered on the far wall.

"Okay." A step stool miraculously appeared where she was looking. "You want me to do it?" he asked innocently.

She wanted him to take a flying hike. "If you were going to do it, you wouldn't have brought out the step stool," she said dryly.

"You need someone to hold the nails," he said helpfully.

She gave in. They bickered back and forth for the

better part of an hour. Greer climbed up and down the step stool forty times to judge the height of the picture, endured no end of comments about her fussiness, paused for a phone conversation with her mother, hammered in the first nail crooked, made a hole in the plaster, suffered his laughter, and triumphantly accepted a glass of wine while they both surveyed the perfectly placed oil painting in shared total exhaustion.

The first sip of wine was sliding down her throat, cool and smooth, when Ryan abruptly murmured, "Stay."

Her eyes darted up to his. The painting behind him abruptly disappeared. Something went wrong with her focus, because the only thing clear in her vision was Ryan. A man with shirtsleeves rolled up and an open collar, a man with brilliant blue eyes and ruffled hair. A man who wasn't smiling. A man who couldn't possibly have playfully patted her fanny moments before when she descended the step stool, because there wasn't an ounce of play in his eyes now. Just wanting. Honest, bold, clear.

In her heart, she'd been expecting that invitation, but not at this particular instant, not after she'd just very foolishly immersed herself in playing wife for the last hour. Lots of clever reasons why she couldn't stay popped into her head. The cat. Stockings to wash out. She'd forgotten to water the plant in her bedroom; she just now remembered it.

Gently, his arms draped over her shoulders, pulling her closer. She couldn't speak; there was something tight and thick in her throat. Maybe the wine. Her cheek rested against his heart a moment later; his arms slowly smoothed around her and he simply held her, length to length, warmth to warmth. He felt so right she could have cried.

"You're going to have to tell me what's bothering

you," he said quietly. "Do you know I love you?"

She shook her head, eyes closed.

"I do, Greer. So much. I love the way you think, your eyes, your legs . . ." He forced her chin up with a smile. "Your sense of humor. I love being beaten by you at chess. I even love your damned cat. And I love . . . touching you." Softly, he stroked her hair back from her forehead with a single finger. "I love doing that, too. Making an absolute mess out of your hair, knowing you don't give a damn. Knowing you care more for the feel of my hands on you than about how you look. Are you going to try to tell me you don't like it when I touch you?"

"No," she said quietly, honestly. Her stricken eyes met his. "You know I do."

"Greer." His finger stayed gently tucked under her chin, his voice grave, gentle. "Has someone hurt you in bed?"

All his subtlety had disappeared, remarkably fast. She should have known. "No, nothing like that." She flushed. The knot in her throat refused to budge. Her palms suddenly felt icy, and she was trembling. "I think . . ." she said hesitantly. "Ryan, I think you want something from me that just . . . isn't there."

The smallest frown furrowed his brow. "You'll have to explain that."

She shook her head. "I don't know how," she said helplessly.

"Honey . . ."

She ducked away from his touch, wrapping her arms around her chest, slowly pacing away from him, and then looking frenetically around the room for her shoes. They weren't in sight. The door, at least, was. Until he slowly, quietly, moved in front of it.

"Look," she said abruptly and took a huge breath,

facing him. "Ryan, I've just never been very good at . . . sexual relationships." She worked frantically to keep her tone light, casual. "Some women are the black-nightgown type, you know? Not me. Caring, loving, listening, showing respect—those are terribly important things to me in a relationship. The . . . other . . . has never really mattered to me." She gulped. "I just feel that . . . that perhaps it would be wiser for us to call it off, not try to go any further. I don't want to disappoint you, and I don't want to be hurt."

"Greer—"

"This is a wonderfully liberated decade. There are lots of women out there who are much more . . . sexual than I am. It's not a question of willingness, or even love." She tried for a smile. "Ryan, I go to bed in a T-shirt with a picture of Garfield on it. Does that tell you anything?"

"Greer—"

"I'll get my shoes another time."

Before the tears could blind her, she whisked past him and out the door, fumbled in the flowerpot for her key, and whipped inside her apartment. She locked the door and leaned against it, her heart pounding, her eyes moist, her hands shaky.

She was terrified he would come after her, but he didn't. After several long minutes of just standing there with her head thrown back against the door, she bit her lip and moved through the dark apartment to turn on a light.

The telephone jangling next to her ear made her jump. She grabbed it, for once with no fear of her crank caller, her only purpose in stopping the mind-splitting noise— or for that moment it seemed mind-splitting.

Her caller didn't wait for her to say hello.

"I love Garfield," said the low voice, "and the rest, sweetheart, is bull."

He hung up.

# Chapter Ten

As Greer left her apartment the following morning, she heard the sound of coughing through Ryan's closed door. She hesitated a moment and then hurried on to work. *You have to stop making him your business, Greer. Besides, he was perfectly healthy last night.*

She worried about him the entire day. When she arrived home just after five, she saw that his car was already parked in the lot, and frowned on her way up the walk. He *never* came home from work before six.

Inside, she changed into a yellow cotton sundress, fed the cat, and fussed with a casserole. She was halfway through dinner when the phone rang. Biting her lip, she rose from the table and determinedly stalked toward the living room.

She picked up the phone on the second ring. "Hello?"

Her eyes squeezed closed when she heard the familiar low, throaty pant. Her stomach curled, and the same old fear licked up her spine. Her hands went slippery as she started to replace the phone. It hadn't quite connected when she heard something else, and lifted the receiver halfway to her ear again.

". . . and get the ** ** ** *hell* off that phone!" The colorful litany was punctuated by a sneeze.

She stared blankly at the receiver for a moment. "Ryan? If you're talking to me—" she started irritably.

"Of *course* I'm not talking to you, foolish one. And *don't* pick up the phone again tonight." He slammed down his end.

She dropped hers. When or if The Breather had dropped his, she had no idea.

She stood silent, for an instant almost smiling. Ryan had quite an extensive vocabulary. She was familiar with all the words but had never heard them strung together in quite that way. She didn't think it was physically possible for The Breather to do with himself what Ryan had suggested.

Her smile abruptly died. Her neighbor was sick. It wasn't just one little cough and a few sneezes that convinced her, but the grating hoarseness in his voice. Abruptly, she whirled for the kitchen, and the freezer.

A half-hour later, with a picnic basket under her arm, she crossed the hall to Ryan's apartment, tentatively set down the basket, and raised her hand to knock. Then dropped her hand, hesitating.

No one could know what it had cost her to admit her sexual failings to Ryan the night before. It had hurt when he refused to take her seriously. There was no way she wanted to give him the least chance to start something

up again. Over a long, sleepless night, she'd decided
that the only way to handle the situation from now on
was to keep her distance.

Still. He was *ill*. And she was hardly *inviting* anything
by just checking on him. When her fingers still hesitated
to knock, she grimly reminded herself that she refused
to play games with him. She was who she was. A lady
who brought cough lozenges, not one who raised blood
pressure. A woman who could be counted on as an honest
friend, not as a potential lover.

She knocked. Once, again, and then a third time.

"Who's there?"

She almost smiled at the crabby voice. "Greer."

"Go away."

She did smile then. The door wasn't locked; she let
herself in. "I'm here," she called out. "Just stay where
you are."

The living room was silent and looked like a general
disaster area. The curtains were closed; the air was stale;
two glasses had been left out from the night before;
clothes were strewn every which way. The kitchen was
deserted, but it looked worse than the living room.

Lugging the picnic basket, Greer ventured determinedly toward Ryan's bedroom and paused in the doorway.

The room looked remarkably different than it had the
night they'd painted it. The king-sized bed was covered
with rumpled cocoa-colored sheets; floor-to-ceiling
bookshelves of natural pecan held a stereo and a smattering of books. A thick comforter in stripes of cream
and dark brown had been tossed on the floor, and he'd
carpeted the room in incredibly plush cocoa that felt like
sponge beneath her feet.

She noticed all of that, but it was the man who really drew her attention, and Ryan looked like hell. Barechested, he was propped up on pillows with a makeshift drawing board in his lap. His hair was all rumpled, his chin dark with whiskers, and his eyes looked glassy and lifeless.

She knew at a glance that he had a fever and that it was high. Dark circles half-mooned beneath his eyes, and there was a white pallor under his tan; dots of moisture marked his brow.

She loved him more that minute than she had ever even conceived of loving anyone. For no reason. Truthfully, he looked tight-lipped and furious when he glanced up and saw her—and the effort of raising his head made him wince, as if he had an excruciating headache.

"Exactly what I expected, McCullough," she said softly. She set down the picnic basket and bent over it, taking items out one by one. "Juice. Soup, nice and hot. Aspirin. Thermometer."

"Take that sweet little fanny of yours out of here, Greer."

She heard the low, rumbled warning, but paid no attention. "If you expect to pull a fit of temper on me, McCullough, you can forget it. When my father gets a sniffle, he can outswear a sailor in a storm. What always kills me about men is that they're at their meanest when they're at their weakest. Machismo comes out of the woodwork, so to speak. Now..." She'd brought glasses as well. Being male, there was every chance he didn't have clean ones. "Lemonade or orange juice?"

"Neither."

"Lemonade it is." She poured a glass and set it next to the bed, efficiently stealing the drawing board from his lap and whisking it to the floor on her downhill swing. "Now, can you handle soup, or is your stomach involved?"

"Your hide is about to be involved. I need to finish that work, and I'd appreciate it if you'd give me back the drawing board. If you value life and limb."

He was propped up against the pillows, his threat virtually groundless. Greer scanned the bed and frowned, her eyes deliberately averted from his Jockey shorts. "Do you own a pair of pajamas?"

"Go home, Greer."

"How long have you had a fever? Did you call the doctor?"

"Go *home*, Greer."

She set the bottle of aspirin next to the lemonade, giving him a wry look. "You're a little testy when you're sick, are you? So am I, McCullough. You're not alone. Take two aspirin and drink the juice. I'll clean up in the other room and bring back some fresh sheets in a few minutes. No arguing."

She heard no protest, and strolled from the room with almost a smile. It felt utterly natural, taking care of him. She didn't really care if he was crabby. And this role, the role of caretaker, came naturally; it was *Greer;* it was her way of showing love and caring, one way she'd always easily shown love and caring.

In the living room, she picked up the dirty dishes and took them to the kitchen. Filling the sink with soapy water, she grabbed a dishcloth and started to work. She wasn't really worried about Ryan. Anyone who had enough energy to be mean couldn't be seriously ill. Actually, she almost felt the silly urge to hum, until the dishcloth was abruptly stolen from her hands by a towering behemoth behind her.

"Ryan, just get back in bed. You shouldn't be up at all. For heaven's sake, I—"

He was pale to his toes, his forehead sweating and his hands unsteady—but not so unsteady he couldn't grasp her by the shoulders and firmly propel her toward the door.

When he flung open the door, he started coughing, but he still managed to push her inelegantly into the hall. "I love you like hell, sweetheart, but I think we'd better get this absolutely straight. For openers, there's no way I'm going to expose you to a virus, even if it's only a twenty-four-hour bug. More important, if I need a mother, I've got one in Maine. There's a hell of a lot I want from you as a woman, lady, but being baby-sat isn't and never will be one of them."

He slammed the door. She heard the latch.

For a moment, she stood stunned. Then she was so furious she couldn't think. The mule-headed dolt. The ungrateful, evil-tempered windbag. For ten cents, she'd send a dozen roses to that mother of his in Maine with a note of congratulations for having survived his upbringing.

In the meantime, she felt as if she'd been kicked in the stomach. Tears stung her eyes as she slammed her own door moments later and immediately crossed the room to take the phone off the hook . . . *not* because she was afraid his rest might be disturbed by one of her telephone calls. Just because.

The two top floors of Charlotte's brand-new Madison Hotel had been transformed for the lingerie trade show. The entire place was covered with froth. Companies from California to Paris had mounted exhibits of panties, nightgowns, bras, teddies, robes, and lounging outfits.

A rainbow of pastels predominated, though there were splashes of scarlet and black as well.

The suppliers outnumbered the designers. Sales reps for manufacturers of cotton, satin, silk, and lace roamed the floors. Industrial sewing machines of many kinds were on exhibit. Thread companies, such as Metrosene from Switzerland, were demonstrating the superior quality and strength of their product. Advertising people were everywhere. The flow of dialogue was 90 percent American slang, with an occasional smattering of French and a few Irish brogues. Though the French didn't like to believe it, Belgian and Irish lace was nothing to sneeze at.

The huge turnout of exhibitors indicated just how big the lingerie industry had become. If the look was frothy, the mood was cutthroat. And by late afternoon on Thursday, Greer had had enough. The razzle-dazzle had had some appeal in the beginning, if for no other reason than that she couldn't possibly think about anything else over the noise, particularly about a nasty-tempered man with fathomless blue eyes.

For once, Ryan was less on her mind than a growing headache. Comparing prices, finding potential new suppliers of fabrics, taking note of quality variations in the industry, comparing the various sewing techniques, trying to gauge trends—she and Ray had work to do here, and both Grant and Marie would expect an extensive report on their return. Only Greer had discovered quickly that fibs and fast lines abounded; talk was cheap and true information difficult to come by.

It wasn't her scene. The constant noise had gotten to her long before dinnertime, when Ray grabbed her arm and suggested a quick and quiet meal in their rooms.

"We shouldn't," Greer said wearily. "This only happens once a year. I promised Marie I would talk to Barteau, and I haven't even seen him..."

"You're entitled to put your feet up, darling. You can track him down tomorrow."

She didn't need much more persuading. A huge yawn escaped her lips as the elevator closed on the two of them. Ray's midnight-dark eyes regarded her with amusement.

"Now I know why I never wanted to go to these things before," Greer admitted. "It would be different if I felt as if I'd accomplished something besides running my feet off."

"You're not supposed to accomplish anything at a trade show. You're supposed to toot your horn and sharpen your nails on the competitor closest to you. You did well," Ray assured her as he led her out on their floor. "Seems foolish for each of us to order room service separately, doesn't it? Your room or mine?"

She paused indecisively, wishing her blasted headache would go away. His room was a long way down the opposite side of the hall. "I suppose mine..." she started uncertainly.

"Fine." He followed her, waited patiently while she fumbled with her room key, and closed the door behind them while Greer collapsed with a sigh of relief in the closest chair.

From her fourth-floor window, she had a view of downtown Charlotte, and her room was lovely. The decor was rose and cream; she had her own couch and chair as well as a large bed and a spacious dressing room, and the maid had put away her carelessly strewn clothes while she'd been working. It was heavenly to be waited on.

Her eyes at half mast, she tilted her head back and curled her feet under her, watching while Ray picked up the phone to dial room service. He was dressed in a dark suit and tie and looked, as usual, sophisticated and ready to seduce, but he'd been very close to an angel this day. He had spared her his usual sexual innuendos and undercurrents. He'd also saved her from a boring lunch with an overbearing advertising executive and had popped up at her side several times during the day with coffee and snacks.

Wearily, she considered getting up to apply fresh makeup, and decided the energy just wasn't there.

Ray put down the phone. "Steaks and wine. Twenty minutes—they claim," he said wryly. "Go ahead. Take off your shoes. Don't tell me you're standing on ceremony because I'm here?"

Wandering toward the window, he was already shrugging off his suit jacket and loosening his tie. He still had energy, Greer marveled, though as always with Ray, it was a restless, uneasy energy. A sudden minuscule tremor touched her spine, the awareness of being alone with him rather catching her by surprise. Foolish. Slipping off her powder-blue pumps, she bent over to rub her aching feet. "We did well, didn't we?" she said lightly. "I thought our booth was as tasteful as any. And from listening to the scuttlebutt, I got the feeling our sales are better than most. What do you think of that new acetate Bingham's is pushing?"

Ray shrugged casually. "I'll take a sample back to Marie."

He didn't want to talk. She couldn't blame him. They'd talked all day. When dinner came, she unbuttoned the jacket of her pale blue suit, tucked her legs under her, and dug in. Room service had delivered the meal on a tea cart, and Ray pushed up to her chair and then sat on the couch across from her.

Twice he leaned over to refill her wineglass. Twice all she could think of was that Ryan did it differently. Ray moved with . . . finesse. Expertise. As if every move had been predetermined by a set of rules. Ryan's body moved with such natural ease . . . but she'd sworn off thinking of Ryan. The man didn't want her around. Not on any basis she was prepared to offer him.

She'd worried about him for three days, which was undoubtedly why she was so wretchedly exhausted after one simple ten-hour period of being on her feet. The relationship . . . was dead. He didn't want a woman who worried about him. He wanted a woman to share his bed. And she knew that just wouldn't work.

An aching loss had trembled through her for three days, but she couldn't have possibly crossed that hall again to make sure he'd recovered from the flu. She'd given up the right to care. Her heart just refused to understand that.

"Why so serious all of a sudden?" Ray teased.

She looked up, embarrassed at not having even offered him companionship over the meal. "Sorry. Woolgathering, I'm afraid."

He pushed the table aside, lifted her full wineglass, and handed it to her. "You were bothered by that man this morning?" he asked casually.

"Jacore?" Greer shook her head. She'd nearly forgotten him. The retailer had expressed interest in Love Lace's products. He'd also cupped a hand on her fanny. When Ray had stepped in, the gentleman had been in danger of losing his hand from the wrist. "No," she said wryly. "Just a little disbelieving anyone could be so crude in front of fifty people."

"You found him particularly . . . offensive, I could tell."

Slightly startled at the odd note in Ray's voice, Greer

glanced up. "He wasn't worth fussing over," she said frankly. "Not that I didn't appreciate your running interference, but honestly, I could have handled him."

"I could cheerfully have strangled him."

A little startled, Greer shrugged and took another sip of wine. "He was hardly worth that," she said dryly. "And I expected some of that kind of thing when I came here."

"You have a lot of men pursuing you. I always knew that."

A second wave of uneasiness traveled down her spine. She wasn't sure why. Ray was perfectly at ease. He'd finished his wine, had poured her another glass—good heavens, her third?—and had stood up to stretch. He leaned back against the wall, his hands loosely in his pockets, his eyes on her. Enigmatic dark eyes.

Her own gaze darted distractedly around the room. "I think I lost the schedule. Tomorrow, the activities start at eight thirty or ni—"

"Were you afraid, when Jacore made that pass?" Ray interrupted silkily.

A small knot settled in her stomach. "Not really." She set down her glass. "Listen. If you remember tomorrow's schedule—"

"You had no need to be afraid. I was watching you the whole time. If any man had dared to give you trouble, Greer, I would have been there."

"I—thank you." She'd definitely had enough of the subject.

"You and I . . ." He hesitated. "We haven't always gotten along. I've never been sure why. I have been wanting to tell you for a long time that I find you—"

"Ray," Greer said abruptly, and stood up. Her room suddenly had dark corners. Charlotte's night lights winked on and off outside the windows, but those lights were a long distance away. "You can go back downstairs tonight if you want, but I'm going to call it a night so I'll be fresh for tomorrow."

He didn't move from his lounging position against the wall. "I think," he said softly, "that you're afraid of something. You've been afraid for some time now. You can tell me, Greer. I'll take care of it for you."

"What on earth are you talking about?" Greer gave a small laugh and heard the sound of her own nervousness. Silly, silly, silly, but she glanced at the door. And silently, like a cat, Ray moved from his position against the wall to a spot between Greer and the only exit.

"I've thought for a very long time," he said quietly, "that you were the kind of woman who needed a strong man. A protective man. A man who would keep you safe from others who want to use you. A lot of men have coveted that beautiful body, haven't they, Greer?"

She was having a nightmare. That was all. It had been a thoroughly exhausting day. Perhaps she had finished dinner and Ray had left and she'd fallen asleep and suddenly she was dreaming. Because she was suddenly afraid of the man standing in front of her to the depths of her bones. A man she had known for five years, who had bothered and annoyed and even distressed her, but who had never threatened any harm to her. She had to be imagining it.

"Tell me," he said quietly.

"Tell you what?" Greer folded her arms across her chest, moving a little away from him on stocking feet. She smiled. Happily. "Dinner was terrific. I'm sorry I was such bad company. Perhaps in the morning..."

"Tell me what you've been afraid of. I can make it go away, Greer. In fact, I'm the only man who can make it go away. And all you have to do is ask me."

"Look," she said firmly. He took a step forward; she couldn't help herself from taking a step back. He smiled.

This was *Ray,* she tried to tell herself. A man she knew well. A man she saw and worked with every day.

"There was a man in the office the other day." Ray's voice was soothing, low, hypnotic. "He's not for you, Greer. All this time, I've pictured you with men. But not him. You think he could stop what you're afraid of? You think he could protect you from *anything?* All this time, have you once *looked* at me?"

"I want you to go," Greer whispered. "Please, Ray." He took another step forward. "Actually, I've regained all my energy," she said brightly. Her voice cracked, and she tried again. "I think I'll just go downstairs and—"

He was close to her now. His hands reached out to grab her shoulders, and Greer froze, her arms still tightly wrapped around her chest.

*"Look,"* she said. "I'm in love with someone else—"

He paid no attention. In slow motion, his face seemed to come toward hers, dark eyes gleaming, dry lips parted. His mouth suddenly groped for hers, and the texture of it felt strange, startling, alien. It was a simple pass. Greer had coped a thousand times with simple passes, but for some unknown reason, this time she was terrified, her body locked in shock.

"Please," she whispered.

"You're not afraid with my arms around you, are you, Greer? I would never, never hurt you . . ."

His mouth lowered again. She turned her head. His body was trying to press against hers. There wasn't that much he could do with the barrier of her arms, but she still felt the contact of her breasts against his white shirt.

And that contact brought a low gush of breath from Ray, and nausea for Greer.

"Ray. Look," she said shakily, "maybe you've had too much wine. We'll forget this, okay? I understand. Only please, just—"

"Just relax," he whispered. "Just relax, Greer. Let it happen. So naturally, it will happen. All this time . . ."

She turned her head, and his lips landed on her throat. Greer jerked convulsively, her arms whipping out like flaying fan blades. *"Don't.* Just get out of here. *No."*

His arms tightened around her like cold bars. A rush of impressions exploded in her head. His hand on her breast, his black eyes with a devil's light, the terrible silence of the room, their isolation, rage, fear, vulnerability, the single burning lamp on the table near the bed.

She twisted free, hearing her own frantic breath.

"The door is locked," he said gently. *"Relax,"* he murmured. "You think I would hurt you? Never, Greer. I can take away what you're afraid of. I'm the only man who can make it completely go away."

He kept talking about that. What she was afraid of. If that was supposed to make sense, it didn't. The only thing she was terrified of was *him.* "Ray. You know me. We've worked together for a long time." Greer swallowed again, as he took another step toward her. "You're an attractive man, but I don't want this kind of—please. I'm sure you'll find someone else . . ."

A low, shivery laugh. Greer darted for the door. His hand slammed against the wood even as she was fighting with the lock. She managed to release the chain, but couldn't reach the knob.

There was a sick scream in the back of her throat, trying to get out, but she remained silent. How could she scream? This couldn't be happening to her. It really couldn't. Maybe if she'd invited it . . . but she knew she *hadn't* invited it. She knew she'd in no way encouraged Ray. As an adolescent, she'd blamed herself for inviting the gropes and grabs that had scared her witless, believing she must have unconsciously asked for trouble. Then during her entire adult life, she'd protected herself by denying every damn possible sexual feeling—and she *hadn't* invited Ray.

His hands were suddenly everywhere, grabbing at her blouse, groping for her skirt. Greer felt a rage suddenly explode inside her. A rage almost as old as she was. It wasn't *her*. It was *him*. Dammit. Had he felt this way about her all along?

His voice rasped in a low, heavy bass. "You like it a little rough, do you, darling?"

Her knee failed. Her fist didn't.

He jerked back, bent suddenly double; a hoarse cry of pain escaped from his mouth.

Greer opened the door, and backed away. "Get out. Now."

# Chapter Eleven

THE MINUTE RAY was gone, Greer pushed the lock button and then fumbled frantically to hook the chain. The room was so silent that she should have felt relieved. Instead, her limbs started trembling as if she'd just been tossed into the Arctic Ocean.

She couldn't get warm. She ran her hands up and down her arms; it didn't help. Her teeth were actually chattering. She walked to the bathroom, turned on the hot water, and splashed some on her face. *He's gone,* the voice in her head assured her. She was *safe.*

Only her heart couldn't seem to stop pounding, and when she turned off the water, her white face stared back at her from the mirror. She winced, seeing the top button gone from her blouse, her skirt askew, the sick glaze in her dark eyes.

She turned away from the mirror, hurrying out of the blouse and her skirt, bundling them both up in her hands. A moment later, she was under the pelting spray of the shower, turned on as hot as her skin could take it. It warmed her up, but when she stepped out, she grew cold again.

She'd brought a cotton robe with her to the conference, and after she wrapped that around her, she dragged the blanket from the bed, draped it over her shoulders, and curled up in the chair. If there was a thought in her head, she couldn't bring it into focus. If she could just get warm . . . She doubted she would ever be warm again. It seemed the only thing that mattered.

When she heard a quiet knock on the door, her whole body went rigid.

Another knock.

When she didn't answer, Ryan's jaw tightened. "Greer. It's Ryan, and I know you're in there. Open the door."

*"Ryan?"*

He waited, an endless period of time. He was pushing his hand through his hair for the dozenth time in the last three hours when the door finally opened.

He'd never seen such a fragile smile in his life. Her hair was damp and had the look of having been rapidly finger-combed. She was wearing a pink cotton robe that buttoned to the neck. Her face was pasty white, with twin spots of color in her cheeks, and he didn't wait to see any more.

He bolted inside, slammed the door behind him, and gathered her immediately in his arms. She was tense and cold, and suddenly her whole body was shuddering.

"I could hardly believe—what on earth are you do-

ing here? How did you even know where I was? And
why—"

"Hush, honey." Her violent shuddering tore at his
heart. His palm cradled her head, pushing her cheek to
his shoulder. His other hand gently caressed her shoulders
and back, kneading, massaging those terribly tense muscles. Finally, some of that shaking stopped, and she lay
quiescent against him.

"Greer." His voice was quiet and infinitely tender, but
there was unquestionably a demand for an answer in his
low, vibrant tone. "Did he scare you? Or . . . hurt you?"

"No, nothing like that. I . . ." Greer lifted her head to
stare at Ryan. If she could just stop feeling so terribly
disoriented . . . Ryan looked exhausted. Taut furrows of
strain aged his features; lines seemed embedded on his
face that hadn't existed days before. His striped shirt was
wrinkled; he was wearing suit pants but no coat. He was
beautiful. And she was so desperately glad to see him
that she could hardly think of anything else. Confusion
suddenly darkened her eyes. "You're over the flu? I was
so worried."

A fleeting look of surprise and almost humor touched
his eyes and then his eyes skimmed past her and around
the room. His jaw clenched when he saw the covered
dinner cart, and his arms first tightened, then soothed.
She felt the gentle sweep of his hand, pushing back her
hair, combing through it. "Would you mind not worrying
about *me* for the moment?" he murmured.

He planted a single kiss on her mouth. A firm kiss,
which seemed to bring a troubled world back into focus
again. And when he lifted his head, she found herself
inches away from clear blue eyes, blue like ice, blue like
fire. "You *knew!*" she whispered suddenly. "When you
just asked me if I was scared, I . . . how could you pos-

sibly have any idea what just happened?"

"I'll explain everything in a little bit. Just tell me what did happen first."

He didn't let her go. He moved her determinedly away from the door, but he kept an arm around her shoulder, and he paused more than once to press his lips on her forehead, her neck, anywhere he could reach. His hands went to her waist, lifting her.

She'd thrown the blanket on the bed. He took it, covering her even as he half carried, half propelled her down onto the pillows. He reached down to push off his shoes, and then came to her.

"I was so *frightened* . . ." Her voice seemed to be coming from miles away.

"Yes." He wound his arms around her and just held her. If he could have wrapped her up in his body, he would have. She'd stopped trembling, and there were suddenly tears.

"I have *never* in my entire life behaved like such a fool."

He didn't contradict her. He didn't do anything to stop the tears or to still the suddenly frantic rush of words. He slid his arm under her waist, covered her again with the blanket, and lay down next to her.

"You don't understand," she said frantically.

"Tell me."

"We were getting along so well. We never had. I thought if I tried to be more understanding—and it was working. I mean, he made sexual remarks all the time, but I never paid any attention. He *knew* I wasn't interested in him; he *had* to know." Images flooded her mind and then receded. "I don't see how he could possibly have misinterpreted anything I'd said or done."

"Greer . . ."

"*No*. It must have been my fault."

"It was *not* your fault," he said emphatically.

"It was. So stupid," she said incoherently. "From the time I was a kid . . . you can't possibly understand. I just *hated* it. I grew up faster than the other girls; they all resented me, but the boys started getting interested in me. Dammit, that's where it all became so confused, and it wasn't something I could talk about with anyone. I didn't want all that attention just because I filled out a bathing suit." She looked at Ryan fiercely, through blurred eyes.

His thumb gently brushed away that film of tears.

"I figured it was my fault," she said softly.

"*Nothing*," he repeated, "was your fault."

"I figured I'd *invited* it. So I stopped . . . *feeling*. It was supposed to be a protection, only it didn't protect me at all. I swear I *never* felt anything for Ray."

"I know that, love," Ryan murmured.

"This evening," she said. "You can't possibly know how I felt. It seemed as if something inside me snapped when he grabbed me. I don't know how to explain. He didn't hurt me. He didn't even touch me intimately. But after blaming myself for so long, I realized suddenly that I wasn't responsible. Except for pretending Ray wasn't a problem. I'd pretended that as long as *I* didn't feel anything, I was safe. If I'd just opened my eyes, I might have seen what was coming . . ."

He grasped the essence of her pain. It took a long time, because she wasn't talking coherently and because the source of her pain had never been clear to him before. It wasn't just Ray she was talking about, but herself and the whole gamut of pent-up feelings she'd experienced: She resented being desirable. She'd run an emotional gauntlet all her life because she was sexually attractive to men who were too insensitive to care about her as a person. She'd felt she had to separate love from sexual feelings.

For the first time in his life, he felt helpless. He'd taken off from work for the last few days, using the excuse of flu, but the virus hadn't actually kept him in bed. He'd been a busy man. He'd been determined to find out the identity of her caller, and he'd accomplished exactly what he'd set out to do, but the only thing that mattered now was Greer. He had to be careful; in no way must he hurt her more.

He listened awhile longer and then leaned over her to switch out the light. Her voice had faded to an exhausted murmur, dropping off completely when darkness covered them. No matter how tired she was, he knew she wasn't even close to sleeping. He could feel the tension in her body even through the covering blanket. And his eyes didn't have to adjust for him to find her mouth in the darkness.

His lips pressed gently, insistently, on hers. His tongue stole between her teeth, filling the moist hollow of her mouth, infusing her with his taste, his warmth, his love for her. His hands swept along her back, outside the blanket that covered her, and he could feel her whole body suddenly grow still.

"Ryan—"

"You don't want this," he murmured, guessing her words before she said them.

"I just..."

"Want to know something, love?"

He raised himself up on an elbow, releasing the buttons of his shirt as he looked down at her. Greer could barely see him in the shadows, but she had a fleeting feeling that he'd catch her if she tried to run. "What?"

"I want to hold you more than I want to make love to you. Now, that hasn't happened often since I met you," he whispered wryly, but there was no smile on his mouth. Just those bright eyes of his burning on hers in the dark. "But we're going to have to make love, Greer. Not for me, love. In fact, I think we'll just forget all about what I want or need. This one's all for you, and you need to understand that ahead of time."

"Ryan—"

"You are beautiful, Greer. Your feelings are beautiful, too, and it's time you believed that. Actually, it's a perfect time, because you're absolutely sure you'll feel nothing, aren't you? You aren't in the mood; you've been frightened to death; and maybe you'd even like to curl up in a corner, honey, but that's not the way."

His shirt dropped to the floor in a gentle woosh. His belt followed. Greer swallowed. "That's just it," she said hesitantly. "I really . . . not now, I—"

He pushed aside the blanket and drew her to him. Blood pulsed in the vein in her throat, in her temples. He was bare from the golden slope of his shoulders to the iron wall of his chest. The room was not so dark now. Her eyes had adjusted, and faint city lights glowed through the windows, illuminating the distinctive shape of a man looming over her.

A very determined man. A few hours earlier, another very determined man had tried to hurt her, but the association was entirely different. This was Ryan. There could never be a comparison. She felt weak inside, unable to stop him or even try, yet suddenly a thousand times more vulnerable than she'd ever felt with Ray or any other man. Ryan's chest with its mat of hair pressed against her as he leaned closer, his mouth claiming hers, stealing her breath, stealing her will to think.

At first her lips only reluctantly returned the pressure, and then, suddenly, fiercely molded themselves to his, her throat arched back to ensure that the bond wasn't broken. When he heard the sudden, uneven rhythm of her breathing, he slowly raised his head. His eyes searched hers. Without looking down, he gently undid the buttons of her robe, from her throat down to her thighs. Just as gently, his hands parted the material. She felt air on her breasts, an awareness of her nakedness, a catch somewhere deep inside her.

Finally, his eyes released their hold on hers and skimmed slowly over her dusk-tipped breasts, the hollow between, the satiny flatness of her stomach. When she raised a hand to cover herself, he held that hand and drew it back to her side.

"You're exquisite," he whispered.

She flushed.

"And that's all we're going to do, honey. Teach you what a beautiful body you have and how beautiful your feelings for me are. No one's going to use you, Greer. Do you know what I want you to do?"

"Ryan—"

"Do you know what I want you to do?" he demanded.

"What?"

"Lie there. That's all. You can think about every damn man who's tried to use you, if you want to. You can repress every sexual feeling you've ever had. And it's still going to happen, love."

He was so serious—and then not. His sudden smile distracted her. She wasn't expecting . . . play. He was most insistent on teaching her that play was part of loving. She couldn't anticipate where he was going to touch next. One moment his lips were tugging at her breasts,

his tongue swirling her nipples into swollen arousal. The
next moment he was trailing kisses up and down her
thigh, and then he moved up, as if he'd completely forgotten the hollow spot in her neck and was making
amends.

He turned her over. He kissed her ankle, the back of
her knee, the soft flesh of her thigh. He nipped at her
bottom, and his tongue laved a long trail up her vertebrae.
When he shifted her to face him after that, he was more
than content to discover her body was becoming Silly
Putty for him. That she sounded breathless as well was
its own reward.

It seemed a good time simply to kiss her senseless.
She murmured something against his mouth, but he didn't
pay any attention. Her limbs were trying to wrap themselves around his; that was message enough.

He took a moment to remove the rest of his clothes,
and when he lay back down on the bed he didn't touch
her at all but just looked at her, from the crown of her
head to the tips of her toes. Moonlight turned her ripe
curves to silver, and her eyes looked as soft as lake water.
So vulnerable. "Listen," she murmured. "I'm not sure.
I warned you, I . . ."

But he'd been listening to Greer for weeks. He wasn't
interested in listening any longer, nor did he want to play.
He had other things to show her. Leaning over her, he
pinned one of her legs with his, loving the feel of his
muscular thigh against her softer one. She had incredibly
beautiful breasts, full and plump and satin smooth. With
infinite slow care, he circled each with a fingertip, then
with his tongue. Her breasts were oh-so-sensitive; he'd
discovered that before. The limits of that sensitivity were
what he needed to know now.

Her nipples were dark brown pebbles. He rolled each tenderly between thumb and forefinger, then bent to taste the right one, teasing it with his tongue, then very gently applying his teeth.

She convulsed, her spine arching for him. He held her closer, allowing her less movement, pinning her hands to her sides. The other nipple he gave different treatment. He laved it to a swelling erection, blew on it to cool it, took it in his mouth to gently suckle.

Greer's thighs tightened around his. He could feel her fingertips pressing down on his spine, but he paid no attention. He pressed her breasts together and kissed the cleavage he'd made. He kneaded the flesh, then massaged it, then traced fingertip patterns over and over those soft, swollen orbs. When he got around to it, he raised his eyes to hers again.

"Damn you, McCullough," she whispered.

He smiled. "I haven't even started, sweet."

She wanted him. She wanted him in the most wanton way; she wanted him as she'd never conceived of wanting anyone. It wasn't . . . nice. He was clearly determined to drive her out of her mind, and if he'd just let her touch him in return . . .

Her hand slid down his stomach, finding him. Ryan just that quickly removed her hand. "Not this time," he murmured. "I'm a little too susceptible to being touched right now, love. Particularly to *your* touch. And there's no way I want to be distracted from just . . . loving you. Not this time."

She raised her hand again.

He said roughly, *"No."*

He looked so fierce. And his fingers drew such delicate patterns over her ribs, down her stomach. A finger traced the soft curl of hair between her thighs; she shivered helplessly. His mouth came up to hers, softening her unwilling cry as his finger probed her flesh. One finger, then two.

It wasn't what she knew of loving, that fierce almost angry need. It was frighteningly full, consuming. She'd denied it for so long; she was burning with it, moving against his hand, feeling his palm against her softness, his finger relentless inside her.

A flame burst, then another. She buried her face in his shoulder, her lips pressed fiercely into his flesh. "Enough," she whispered.

He stopped after a time—only, really, to smile at her. "You have miles to go, if you think that's all there is to pleasure, love," he murmured. "Honey, I think you have to accept that you aren't going to get any sleep tonight."

"Greer."

"Hmm."

"You're *not* going to sleep yet."

Ryan watched her open one sleepy eye, lift her head to look at him vaguely, and then let her cheek flop back onto his chest.

"Ryan. I *am* asleep. You make a very good mattress," she murmured.

"Thank you."

"Am I cutting off your circulation?"

"Sweetheart, you cut off my circulation around three hours ago."

"You should have said something."

"Why? I want you just where you are." His palm trailed a lazy path down her bare spine. "Now, don't drop off again. We have unfinished business."

The woman sprawled across his body like an abandoned waif had been exactly the sensual lover he'd known she could be. Actually, she'd proved an incomparable hedonist. She loved touching, and being touched.

But she certainly didn't wake up easily. Even when his finger trailed up her side and she jerked away from his tickling, all he got was a momentary dour scowl and a sleepy yawn. "Business," she echoed vaguely. "Actually, we do have business, don't we? You never did say how you happened to be here. How you knew about Ray, why you drove all this distance—"

"Not *that* kind of business. We can talk about all that tomorrow. I meant important stuff." Locking his arms around her, he rolled her over and stole the pillow from behind her head, tossing it on the floor.

Her eyes looked up at him disbelievingly. "You can't still have the energy."

"I didn't hear you say it."

"Say what?"

"I want to hear you say how beautiful you are. I want you to say, 'Ryan, I am a very sexy lady and I'm not embarrassed about it.'" His lips brushed hers fleetingly. "You *are* beautiful, you know."

"Ryan."

"The thing is, I need to know that you feel beautiful about yourself."

She parted her lips and then hesitated, her eyes luminous on his, fully awake. "It was you," she whispered. "It's the way you make love to me, the way you make me feel."

He shook his head. "Nice. Not good enough, but nice." His palm cupped her breasts, then slipped down her stomach to the parting of her thighs. She responded immediately, her arms sliding around him, pulling him closer. "Are you going to say it for me?" he whispered.

"I can't *say* something like that. I'd sound like an egotistical maniac."

He sighed. "In some ways, you're an extremely slow learner. You've obviously completely missed what I was trying to teach you. We'll have to try again."

"Will we?" she asked wryly.

"And you're not going to get any sleep tonight until you tell me how beautiful you are."

"I haven't gotten any sleep so far. There doesn't seem to be a great deal of difference," she whispered wryly.

She was wrong, she discovered very quickly. Ryan had made love to her in ways she'd never thought of, seeking ways of giving her pleasure that had left her breathless, and tearful, and exultant. Her body seemed to belong to someone else. She was sensitive where she hadn't known she was sensitive, responsive in ways she'd never believed she was responsive.

He hadn't once claimed his own satisfaction. In some mystical way, as he knelt over her, as he probed that core of her in the timeless way of man and woman, she looked into his eyes and knew he still wasn't claiming her for his own pleasure.

She forgot the thought for a minute. He felt infinitely good inside her. She shuddered everywhere, within, without, all over, as he slid in and out in a slow, lazy rhythm. A rush of sweet yearning started to build, and his rhythm changed, quickened, feeding the greedy sensuality he'd taught her earlier.

"Tell me," he whispered.

He lifted her closer to him, his palms on her bottom encouraging a deeper fit. He filled the hollow inside her, a hollow that seemed to reach as far as her heart.

She'd already discovered he was a man without mercy,

but this time she also discovered that Ryan could be a heartless tease. The pleasure he'd given so freely he now withheld. He touched with love and he touched with tenderness, one moment claiming her as a pagan would claim his captive after battle, the next soothing her with a sensual serenade in which his movements were the rhythm and his whispers were the melody. He urged her to feel. Everything.

She felt. Everything. And he would completely withdraw just when she was certain the pinnacle loomed before her. Her body grew as slippery as his, feverishly hot, yet the man refused to yield control.

"Tell me," he whispered.

"I'm beautiful," she hissed desperately.

"Exquisite."

"Exquisite."

"Incomparably sensual. And loving it."

She gathered she was supposed to repeat that, too. She raised her head, sealed his mouth closed with her own, and sent her fingernails running down his spine.

After that, there wasn't much talking.

# Chapter Twelve

". . . SO YOU HAVE the right to press charges, ma'am."

Greer stared in confusion at the polite uniformed officer standing in front of her with his hat in his hand. "I still don't understand," she said uncertainly.

Bright sunlight was pouring in the windows of Grant's office. It was one o'clock on Friday afternoon. Grant was sitting behind his desk, looking at her, and Marie was pacing by the windows, furiously trying to send some message to Greer with hand motions.

"The most he'll likely get is a fine. Nuisance calls are only a misdemeanor. Also, nobody seems to have seen him since last night. I'm not saying that he's necessarily skipped town, but his place looks pretty empty of clothes and other personal things. We can probably track him down, but we need to know for sure whether or not you want to press charges. Miss?"

Greer saw Marie frantically nod her head, but she pushed her hands in the pockets of her dirndl skirt and leaned back against the wall. "No," she said quietly.

Grant rose from his chair to escort the policeman out a few moments later, then closed his office door on the way back in. "Sit down, Greer," he suggested.

Gratefully, she sank into the chair closest to his desk. Her legs felt numb. Actually, her whole body felt numb. "I can't believe Ray was the one who made those calls," she murmured. "I just can't believe it."

The whole morning had been disastrously confusing, partly because she'd had very little sleep. Ryan had had none at all; he'd left the hotel in Charlotte at five to drive back to work. She couldn't drive back with him; there were still a few ends to clean up from the trade show, and she had her car besides. Ray had disappeared, but she hadn't expected to walk into work this afternoon and discover he'd been fired. And before she'd had the chance to level a single question at Grant, the policeman had called from the lobby. She was still trying to absorb one shock, and then there was another.

Marie bounced in front of her, jangling bracelets dancing on her wrists as she pointed a scolding finger at Greer. "When I think of what that man put you through," she said viciously, "I could kill him. And *you*. *You* should have immediately called us after what happened at the trade show. *And* pressed charges." Still clucking like a mother hen, she whirled behind Greer to her husband's credenza, immediately bringing back a cup of hot tea for Greer.

Greer put both hands around the warm cup gratefully,

took a single sip, and set it down. With haunted eyes, she stared at Grant. "I made him lose his job?" she said quietly. "I can't seem to get any of this straight. He actually *told* you what happened in my hotel room? And he admitted the truth about the phone calls besides?"

Marie and Grant exchanged glances. "I fired Ray," Grant said quietly, "for sexually harassing an employee. There's no possible way I would have allowed him back here after what he did to you. I have the right to fire any employee for misconduct. Ray was my employee and acting as a representative for Love Lace every moment he was at the trade show. And frankly, we've been looking for an excuse to let him go for some time."

"I don't understand," Greer said, bewildered. "I thought he always did an outstanding job."

"He brought in a great many sales, yes, which is why we kept him for so long, but he didn't get along with anyone, except maybe you. He couldn't relate to people. Customers complained about him all the time; Tim has all but quit several times after one of their confrontations."

"I didn't know," Greer said unhappily.

"His references looked impressive when I hired him. So impressive that I was foolish enough not to check. Yesterday, I made several phone calls to places he'd previously worked, and discovered that he was fired from each of those jobs." Grant sighed. "Ray is ambitious and hardworking, but something is driving the man. Nothing's ever enough. He always has to outdo the people he works around, and if he can't, he tries subtle intimidation tactics."

"Like those phone calls," Marie said loudly. "I still want to know why you didn't come to Grant or me, darling. You think we don't care about you, that you are nothing but an employee to us? I am so disappointed in you I could scream."

"Marie." Grant's voice was soft, but admonishing.

Greer touched trembly fingers to her temples. "What did I do?" she asked unhappily. "I never . . . threatened him in my job. Why did he pick on me?"

"Because he was a total ass," Marie hissed.

"Perhaps," Grant said quietly, "because you were someone he wanted and couldn't have. It would fit the pattern. Not that I know about his personal life, but in his work, if he couldn't achieve something he wanted, he made sure someone paid. Greer?"

She looked up.

"He was fired from one job for fabricating an elaborate set of reports that would have made another employee look bad. The saddest part about it was that the company wasn't dissatisfied with Ray to begin with. He'd failed to bring in an account; it wasn't the end of the world. He was the one who made trouble for himself."

"He's *sick*," Marie said emphatically. "Sick, sick, sick."

"Sad," Greer corrected in a low voice.

Grant nodded quietly to her over the desk. "He needs help, I expect. Psychiatric help. I told him that when I fired him."

"But . . . how did the police know about the phone calls? And I still don't understand why he told you what happened at the trade show. This morning when I learned he was gone, I assumed that he'd come back here, but—"

"He told us nothing," Marie said heatedly. "Grant fired him over the telephone when Ray called this morning."

"But—"

Grant leaned back in his chair. "Your Mr. McCullough made an extremely informative call to me earlier." A small smile touched his features. "One of several in the last week, actually. After last night, I think he would have preferred to have Ray drawn and quartered, but he settled for explaining to me exactly what Ray had put you through. McCullough also persuaded me to make those reference checks yesterday. And he convinced the police to tap Ray's phone last week. Unfortunately, they didn't get a report back on that until yesterday."

*"What?"* Marie turned offended eyes to her husband. "You told me nothing about that part of it."

But Grant was looking only at Greer. "Mr. McCullough had reason to believe that one of our employees was your caller. You changed your phone number twice; yet your caller knew that new number each time—and, of course, you immediately informed *us* of your new telephone number each time. Except for your family, who could have learned your number and your personal schedule so quickly, except someone you worked with?"

Grant's voice was soothing, quiet. Greer had always found her boss's voice gentling. Not this time.

Her thoughts were filled with Ryan. He'd done all of that. And he hadn't said a single word.

Grant and Marie both urged her to take the rest of the afternoon off and go home. She didn't. She wanted to think, and always thought best when she was busy. Mulling over a problem while facing four walls and total silence always sounded good, but it never worked for Greer.

She left several minutes before five, though. Ryan, of course, wasn't back from work when she arrived at the apartment. She didn't expect him to be. After running a brush through her hair, she left her door open and paced up and down the hall, Truce pacing directly behind her.

Ryan didn't pop through the door until ten to six, early for him. He was dressed strictly as a businessman, in a pale gray suit that made his shoulders look huge, and was reaching for the newspaper when he noticed her at the top of the steps. She was standing stiff as a board, with her arms folded over her chest, eyes blazing.

He froze.

Greer's eyes pinned him as securely as a collector pins a moth. "I would appreciate the chance to talk with you," she said crisply. "I discovered exactly how much you were involved in getting Ray . . . caught."

"Greer . . ." He took a very careful breath, eyes on her face. "You're upset because I interfered. I don't blame you, but try to understand. I didn't want to go behind your back, but I knew damn well you'd say no if I asked you ahead of time."

"You bet I'm upset. And as I said, I'd like to talk with you, McCullough. Like in an hour. Your place."

"Greer . . ."

She turned on her heel, whirled into her apartment and locked the door. Truce screamed. She opened the door, let the cat bound in, and relocked it.

Her heart shifted promptly into *race,* as though a computer button had suddenly been turned on. She flipped off one shoe, then the other, then padded barefoot toward the bathroom, unbuttoning her shirtwaist dress as she went. The pale lavender cotton dropped somewhere in the hall, and she left it there. By the time she turned on the shower taps, she was wearing only bra and pants, and she stripped those off as the shower warmed up.

Ten minutes later, she stepped out, fiercely rubbed her hair with a towel until it was half dry, then used a blow dryer and brush to do the rest. Naked, she walked to her bedroom and bent down over her lowest dresser drawer.

It was there. The cream lace on pink satin negligee. Her quick-quick movements slowed abruptly. Her fingers took the time to caress the soft fabric before she drew it out. *Really, Greer. This is terribly out of character.*

And her heart was suddenly beating erratic rhythms. Old ghost rhythms.

For so long, she'd valued the safe niche she'd carved out for herself in her relationships with men. "Safe" was being a friend, not a lover. "Safe" meant caretaking and playing with men only when she was in control. "Safe" had been convincing herself that that was what she was as a woman, and all she was and wanted to be.

Ray had blown her definitions of "safe" off the map.

Ryan had made her see what she wanted and needed for herself as a woman.

Slowly, she slipped the satin over her head, and with a whisper it draped itself over her body and fell in long, sleek lines to the floor. Ryan had taught her a lesson in honesty. Now it was up to her to put his teachings into practice.

Fingers suddenly trembling, she drew on the cream lace peignoir that matched the negligee, and caught her reflection in the mirror. A boldly sexual woman stared back at her. An alluring woman. Her breasts were barely covered by the cobwebby bodice; she could see the dark tips of her nipples. Lower, she could even see the indentation of her navel: satin *did* show everything. Every curve, each line of her bottom and thighs, even the small raised mound that was the woman of her.

She sprayed perfume on her throat, then between her breasts and, with wildly shaking fingers, between her thighs. The perfume cooled, raising goose bumps on her skin. Leaning over the dresser, she brushed an almost imperceptible layer of mascara on her lashes and a subtle blush on her cheeks, then bit her lips to make them red.

Even watching herself in the mirror brought color to her cheeks, and she left the room in a rush, making it all the way to the door before she realized her palms were damp from nerves. Impatiently, she backtracked to the kitchen, dried her hands determinedly on a towel, and rubbed some cream on them. It didn't make any particular sense to apply lotion to damp hands, but Greer wasn't acting rationally at the moment.

Old ghosts had to be exorcised. There was a man across the hall who seemed to think she was a sexually vibrant woman. Mostly because he'd brought out that side of her the night before. She'd been a participant then, not an aggressor, and that was the difference. Life just *refused* to be easy.

She opened the door, crossed the hall, took a huge breath, and knocked on her neighbor's door.

The door opened instantly. Ryan had his sleeves rolled up and a drink in his hand. He'd obviously run his fingers through his hair over and over, because that cinnamon-colored mane was impossibly tousled. Worry lines were etched around his deeply troubled eyes, and his mouth was parted to say something immediately when he caught sight of her. Caught sight of *all* of her.

His mouth abruptly closed. He leaned out into the hall and looked one way, then the other. Seeing no one else, he abruptly pulled her inside and out of sight, then slammed the door behind her and put his drink down on a table.

She hadn't breathed yet, not in about the last five minutes as far as she could remember. Ryan leaned against

the door, that frantically worried look only gradually
leaving his face as his eyes slowly skidded over her body
from throat to toe. And then again. And then again.

When his eyes finally traveled up to hers, they were
sky blue, bottomless blue, and filled with love. Greer
desperately, desperately wanted that love, but what she'd
anticipated seeing in his eyes was desire. She had *not*
expected him to shake his head with a scolding grin.
"You knew damn well I was worried as hell when I
walked in and you jumped me. I thought you were angry."

"I *was* angry. With me." Because he'd touched her.
And she'd never touched him. Not the right way. Not in
a way that honestly expressed how much she wanted
him. Not in a way that told him she felt out of control
and lushly wanton like some primal Eve when he kissed
her, when he made love to her. And that really loving
him meant finding the courage to express those feelings.
She moved forward slowly, her eyes not on his face but
on his top shirt button.

It had to go. So did the next. So did the next. He
stood very still while she pressed slow, nuzzling kisses
on his throat and neck. She pulled the shirt out of his
waistband while still kissing him. And as she pushed it
off his shoulders, she rubbed her breasts seductively
against his bare skin. The feeling of Ryan's warm flesh
against her satin-and-lace-clad body was . . . delightful.
Dangerously delightful.

For the first time in her life she was in the mood to
court danger.

His shirt dropped to the floor. Her tongue lapped at
the tiny flat nub on the right side of his chest; her fingers
fumbled with his belt. It wouldn't give. She felt his hand
trying to nudge hers aside and murmured, "No. Let me."

His belt buckle simply wouldn't give. But finally she

loosened it, and then unfastened the waistband of his pants, her lips still trailing kisses on his bare chest. She stopped then, simply to rub against him again, her arms around his neck and her fingers sneaking slowly into his hair. The satin made a small sliding sound, like a whisper, every time there was the slightest friction between the two bodies. Greer was fascinated, creating more friction. And both bodies seemed to be growing warmer.

Ryan said nothing. She would probably have died if he had. He stood so absolutely still, while her fingers lightly slipped down his sides and slid inside his pants, beneath the waistband of his shorts, seeking bare, intimate flesh, finding it. She tried a love bite on his shoulder and marveled at how he responded. So many things she had to know. So many things she wanted to learn about him, instantly.

Her whole body was willing to continue that slow exploration—except for her knees. There was something wrong with her knees. They just didn't want to stand up anymore. Slowly, she raised her eyes to his and murmured softly, "One of us seems to be having a problem with heavy breathing." She hesitated, and then added shakily, "Me."

"A penny for them."

Greer glanced at Ryan next to her and smiled, fluffing the pillow behind her as she shifted to a slightly more comfortable position against the headboard. Her body was bare, and so was Ryan's. The negligee was really in a rather bedraggled heap on the floor; but then, lingerie was the fantasy. Making love, she would never tire of discovering, was real. "I was just wondering," she said pensively, "whether or not I should ask you to marry me."

A crooked smile slashed across Ryan's face. He hadn't been able to keep his eyes off her for the last twenty minutes. He wanted to memorize each feature at this moment. And by the time he'd memorized each one, he wanted to do it again. "Oh?" he questioned.

"There comes a time when a woman has to learn once and for all how to be aggressive," she told him gravely.

"I see." He was diverted momentarily by the curve of her shoulder. He frowned, worried that the spot had been neglected. He leaned over, and his lips closed on that soft flesh.

"You're not paying attention. This is important. I'd like to hear what you think of the idea."

"That depends," he said thoughtfully. "Does the cat come with the proposal?"

"Yes."

"I figured." He sighed. "I don't know, sweet. You already know I can be a little touchy when I'm under the weather..."

"A *little* touchy is an understatement. But after giving that problem due consideration, I decided I can live with it."

"Well. If you can live with that, I guess it comes down to whether or not I can live with the kind of woman you are." His eyes touched hers. Touched, caressed, lingered. "You wore me out, love."

"Did I?"

"I'm not sure I can live up to the challenge of a wantonly seductive temptress with an endlessly creative sex drive. I'd get old before my time."

"True," Greer murmured demurely.

He pulled the pillow out from behind her. Her head plopped flat on the mattress. He leaned over her, lips poised for a kiss that didn't quite happen. "I love you," he murmured. "Despite the cat, despite knowing I'll be worn out by my delectably sexy lady, there isn't any way on earth I could live without you. I knew that a long time ago." He paused, the intensity in his voice softening to a lazy murmur. "Just in case there's any doubt in your mind, that means I accept your proposal. You don't mind if I take my turn at being the aggressive one now, do you?"

Greer feigned a frown, stretching luxuriously beneath him. "I don't know. I was just getting into the spirit of the thing. Being the boss, doing the seducing..."

"We'll take turns," he assured her. "But this one's definitely on me." And then his lips found home.

## Second Chance at Love ®

| | | |
|---|---|---|
| ___ 0-425-08151-6 | GENTLEMAN AT HEART #263 Elissa Curry | $2.25 |
| ___ 0-425-08152-4 | BY LOVE POSSESSED #264 Linda Barlow | $2.25 |
| ___ 0-425-08153-2 | WILDFIRE #265 Kelly Adams | $2.25 |
| ___ 0-425-08154-0 | PASSION'S DANCE #266 Lauren Fox | $2.25 |
| ___ 0-425-08155-9 | VENETIAN SUNRISE #267 Kate Nevins | $2.25 |
| ___ 0-425-08199-0 | THE STEELE TRAP #268 Betsy Osborne | $2.25 |
| ___ 0-425-08200-8 | LOVE PLAY #269 Carole Buck | $2.25 |
| ___ 0-425-08201-6 | CAN'T SAY NO #270 Jeanne Grant | $2.25 |
| ___ 0-425-08202-4 | A LITTLE NIGHT MUSIC #271 Lee Williams | $2.25 |
| ___ 0-425-08203-2 | A BIT OF DARING #272 Mary Haskell | $2.25 |
| ___ 0-425-08204-0 | THIEF OF HEARTS #273 Jan Mathews | $2.25 |
| ___ 0-425-08284-9 | MASTER TOUCH #274 Jasmine Craig | $2.25 |
| ___ 0-425-08285-7 | NIGHT OF A THOUSAND STARS #275 Petra Diamond | $2.25 |
| ___ 0-425-08286-5 | UNDERCOVER KISSES #276 Laine Allen | $2.25 |
| ___ 0-425-08287-3 | MAN TROUBLE #277 Elizabeth Henry | $2.25 |
| ___ 0-425-08288-1 | SUDDENLY THAT SUMMER #278 Jennifer Rose | $2.25 |
| ___ 0-425-08289-X | SWEET ENCHANTMENT #279 Diana Mars | $2.25 |
| ___ 0-425-08461-2 | SUCH ROUGH SPLENDOR #280 Cinda Richards | $2.25 |
| ___ 0-425-08462-0 | WINDFLAME #281 Sarah Crewe | $2.25 |
| ___ 0-425-08463-9 | STORM AND STARLIGHT #282 Lauren Fox | $2.25 |
| ___ 0-425-08464-7 | HEART OF THE HUNTER #283 Liz Grady | $2.25 |
| ___ 0-425-08465-5 | LUCKY'S WOMAN #284 Delaney Devers | $2.25 |
| ___ 0-425-08466-3 | PORTRAIT OF A LADY #285 Elizabeth N. Kary | $2.25 |
| ___ 0-425-08508-2 | ANYTHING GOES #286 Diana Morgan | $2.25 |
| ___ 0-425-08509-0 | SOPHISTICATED LADY #287 Elissa Curry | $2.25 |
| ___ 0-425-08510-4 | THE PHOENIX HEART #288 Betsy Osborne | $2.25 |
| ___ 0-425-08511-2 | FALLEN ANGEL #289 Carole Buck | $2.25 |
| ___ 0-425-08512-0 | THE SWEETHEART TRUST #290 Hilary Cole | $2.25 |
| ___ 0-425-08513-9 | DEAR HEART #291 Lee Williams | $2.25 |
| ___ 0-425-08514-7 | SUNLIGHT AND SILVER #292 Kelly Adams | $2.25 |
| ___ 0-425-08515-5 | PINK SATIN #293 Jeanne Grant | $2.25 |
| ___ 0-425-08516-3 | FORBIDDEN DREAM #294 Karen Keast | $2.25 |
| ___ 0-425-08517-1 | LOVE WITH A PROPER STRANGER #295 Christa Merlin | $2.25 |
| ___ 0-425-08518-X | FORTUNE'S DARLING #296 Frances Davies | $2.25 |
| ___ 0-425-08519-8 | LUCKY IN LOVE #297 Jacqueline Topaz | $2.25 |

Prices may be slightly higher in Canada.

---

*Available at your local bookstore or return this form to:*

**SECOND CHANCE AT LOVE**
*Book Mailing Service*
*P.O. Box 690, Rockville Centre, NY 11571*

Please send me the titles checked above. I enclose _____ Include 75¢ for postage and handling if one book is ordered; 25¢ per book for two or more not to exceed $1.75. California, Illinois, New York and Tennessee residents please add sales tax.

NAME _____

ADDRESS _____

CITY _____ STATE/ZIP _____

(allow six weeks for delivery)                              SK-41b

# COMING NEXT MONTH
## IN THE
## SECOND CHANCE AT LOVE SERIES

**HEARTS ARE WILD #298 by Janet Gray**
High-stakes poker player Emily Farrell never
loses her cool and *never* gambles on love—until alluring
Michael Mategna rips away her aloof façade and exposes
her soft, womanly yearnings.

**SPRING MADNESS #299 by Aimée Duvall**
The airwaves sizzle when zany deejay Meg
Randall and steamy station owner Kyle Rager join
forces to beat the competition...and end up
madly wooing each other.

**SIREN'S SONG #300 by Linda Barlow**
Is Cat MacFarlane a simple singer or a criminal
accomplice? Is Rob Hepburn a UFO investigator or
the roguish descendant of a Scots warrior clan? Their
suspicions entangle them in intrigue...and passion!

**MAN OF HER DREAMS #301 by Katherine Granger**
Jessie Dillon's looking for her one true love—and
she's sure Jake McGuire isn't it! How can a devious
scoundrel in purple sneakers who inspires such
toe-tingling lust possibly be the man of her dreams?

**UNSPOKEN LONGINGS #302 by Dana Daniels**
Joel Easterwood is a friend when Lesley Evans
needs one most. But she's secretly loved him since
childhood, and his intimate ministrations are
tearing her apart!

**THIS SHINING HOUR #303 by Antonia Tyler**
Kent Sawyer's blindness hasn't diminished his
amazing self-reliance...or breathtaking sexual appeal.
But is Eden Fairchild brave enough to allow this
extraordinary man to care for *her*?

# QUESTIONNAIRE

1. How do you rate _____

   (please print TITLE)

   ☐ excellent        ☐ good
   ☐ very good        ☐ fair        ☐ poor

2. How likely are you to purchase another book
   in this series?

   ☐ definitely would purchase
   ☐ probably would purchase
   ☐ probably would not purchase
   ☐ definitely would not purchase

3. How likely are you to purchase another book by
   this author?

   ☐ definitely would purchase
   ☐ probably would purchase
   ☐ probably would not purchase
   ☐ definitely would not purchase

4. How does this book compare to books in other
   contemporary romance lines?

   ☐ much better
   ☐ better
   ☐ about the same
   ☐ not as good
   ☐ definitely not as good

5. Why did you buy this book? (Check as many as apply)

   ☐ I have read other
      SECOND CHANCE AT LOVE romances
   ☐ friend's recommendation
   ☐ bookseller's recommendation
   ☐ art on the front cover
   ☐ description of the plot on the back cover
   ☐ book review I read
   ☐ other _____
      _____
      _____

(Continued...)

6. Please list your three favorite contemporary romance lines.
_____
_____

7. Please list your favorite authors of contemporary romance lines.
_____
_____
_____
_____
_____
_____

8. How many SECOND CHANCE AT LOVE romances have you read? _____

9. How many series romances like SECOND CHANCE AT LOVE do you <u>read</u> each month? _____

10. How many series romances like SECOND CHANCE AT LOVE do you <u>buy</u> each month? _____

11. Mind telling your age?
        ☐ under 18
        ☐ 18 to 30
        ☐ 31 to 45
        ☐ over 45

☐ Please check if you'd like to receive our <u>free</u> SECOND CHANCE AT LOVE Newsletter.

We hope you'll share your other ideas about romances with us on an additional sheet and attach it securely to this questionnaire.

• • • • • • • • • • • • • • • • • • • • • • • • • • • • • • • •

Fill in your name and address below:
Name _____
Street Address _____
City _____ State _____ Zip _____

Please return this questionnaire to:
   SECOND CHANCE AT LOVE
   The Berkley Publishing Group
   200 Madison Avenue, New York, New York 10016